ALSO BY KIMBERLY MULLINS:

Notebook Mysteries ~ Emma (Book 1)

Notebook Mysteries ~ Decisions and Possibilities (Book 2)

Notebook Mysteries ~ Changes and Challenges (Book 3)

Notebook Mysteries ~ Unexpected Outcomes (Book 4)

Notebook Mysteries ~ Haunted Christmas (a novella)

Notebook Mysteries ~ Suspicions (Book 5) -Released
March 2023

Notebook Mysteries ~ Parisian Intrigue (Book 6)- August 2023

Notebook Mysteries ~ A Party to Remember (a Christmas
novella) September 2023

Notebook Mysteries

Notebook Mysteries

A Party to Remember

KIMBERLY MULLINS

NOTEBOOK MYSTERIES ~ A Party to Remember (a novella)

Notebook Mysteries Series

Copyright © JKJ books, LLC 2023

First edition: September 2023

Mailing address for JKJ books, LLC; 17350 State Highway 249, STE 220 #3515 Houston, Texas 77064

Library of Congress Control Number: 2023913285

ISBN (paperback) 979-8-9886080-1-1

ISBN (hardback) 979-8-9886080-2-8

ISBN (ebook) 979-8-9886080-0-4

This is a work of fiction. It is based on historical events within Chicago during the time period of the 1880s.

Edited by Kaitlyn Katsoupis, Strictly Textual

Cover Art by Miblart

Christmas is such a magical time that my family treasures.
To the people I spend Christmas with-Jonathan, Joshua and Sharron.
And to include the person I miss always-Claudia— Merry Christmas!!

PROLOGUE

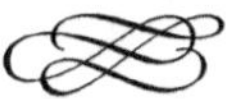

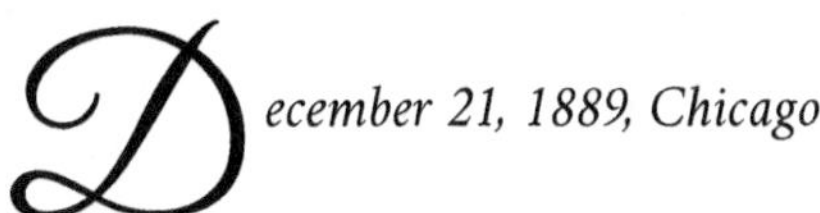

December 21, 1889, Chicago

"Is it finished, Geoff?" the man asked, pacing up and down in a jerky movement behind the other man.

"Yes, Gregory, it is," Geoff said and closed the trunk. The click signaled the finality of what had been done.

"Was this one too close to home?" asked Gregory.

"Yes, but this one is for you," Geoff commented.

He slumped in his chair and muttered, "For me, for me."

Geoff walked to his chair in the dark room. The only lighting was the large Christmas tree in the corner. The candles had been lit, and they cast shadows through the room. He liked the ambiance as he pulled out his cigarette case and chose one to light. "Too close?" he replied. "No, I think it's just right. Especially for this group."

"But why did you have to invite her?" Gregory's voice rose to a higher octave.

"Because we're ready."

Gregory turned his gaze from Geoff to the trunk. "Are we?" he muttered to himself.

CHAPTER 1

A few weeks earlier, December 2, 1889

Slam!

The door hit the wall and drove snow into the house. Along with the snow came a person covered from head to toe in frost. They started to brush themselves off, the flurries covering the floor of the foyer.

"Careful there," Dora said from the sitting room doorway.

"Sorry about that," Emma said as she pushed the door closed. She stayed where she was and knocked the snow off her boots onto the mat. All the while, she hummed the song "Hark! The Herald Angels Sing."

"Now, you can sweep that snow back outside," her sister said as she walked over and handed Emma the broom that had become a fixture in the foyer during the winter season. "You're festive today," she observed.

Emma did as she was told and continued to hum. "I am. I

can't wait for Christmas." When she finished her task, she looked over at Dora. "What're you reading?"

Dora looked up from the envelope she was holding. "An invitation."

"Really, to what?" She walked over to her and looked at the invitation.

" Geoff and Gregory are having their Christmas party in Chicago this year."

"And we're invited? Don't they usually have these in New York or Boston?"

"Yes, I believe so."

"I've always wondered about them. Geoff leaves weeks in advance to get ready and then doesn't return until after Christmas." She studied the invitation. "Who else do you think will be invited?"

Dora held up another envelope. "I'm not sure, but this one is for Savannah."

Emma frowned and stepped back to take her coat off. "Does she know Geoff?" she asked as she removed her hat and patted her hair.

"I'm not sure; we can ask. As for the others, we don't normally travel in the same circles as Geoff."

"No, he's kept to himself since he moved here. You know, his friend Gregory does come by the accounting office occasionally. I think the last time I saw him was last year when we were doing a final audit on the charity's files." Emma took her gear to the closet to hang them up and closed the door.

"Isn't he a pianist?"

She walked back to her sister and took the invitation from her. "Yes, and very talented."

"That might be how he knows Savannah." The sisters' friend Savannah was currently working at the Columbia Theater as a stage manager. Her parents were actors and she had grown up in the theatre world.

"That could be," Emma mused. "He's never accepted our invitations for the charity events."

"We've tried to include him in them or our parties, but he hasn't shown any interest," Dora commented.

"He has always contributed, but he doesn't attend," Emma said absently. "I wonder why now."

"He may be doing it to be polite," offered Dora, "since he's having it in Chicago. Maybe it's a business invitation."

"Maybe," she agreed, though she had her doubts. Geoff had never mentioned anything about the parties he held.

"Do we send in a yes?" asked Dora.

"Let's bring it up over dinner," she suggested.

Dora nodded. "Are you worried about something?"

She grinned suddenly and said, "Jeremy would say that I'm always worried. It might just be what it looks like, an invitation to a party." Dora laughed and took her arm to go into the dining room. "There's something important we should consider."

"What's that?" Dora asked, uneasy her sister may have found a reason for concern about the party.

"What'll we wear?"

She laughed abruptly and said, "We have those dresses from Paris."

"That's true." They'd just returned from Paris where Abbey, Jeremy's mom, had gotten them beautiful dresses.

"If Savannah and Ethan go, we'll have to help her with a dress."

"We have some we could modify for her."

The dinner hour was fast approaching and the table needed to be set.

CHAPTER 2

hat night

The table was always fuller on Monday than any other day. Savannah and Ethan were there for dinner, as Mondays the theatres were closed for the night so that performers and staff could have a day off.

They'd given Savannah the invitation to the party. She opened it as Ethan looked on. "The date," she said, frowning, "isn't it close to the wedding?"

Dora said, "No, not too much; you're getting married on Christmas Eve, so you'll have a few more days to get ready."

Savannah and Ethan shared a glance; he answered for them. "We'd like to talk some first. Can we let you know later?"

"That should be fine. We'll give you a few days to let us know," Dora replied.

"Thanks."

I wonder what the hesitation is? thought Emma. *Just the proximity to the wedding?*

Dinner continued with news and food being passed around the table. Jeremy leaned over to Emma and whispered in her ear, "Any thoughts on the party?"

"You know me so well," she teased. "I find it odd we were invited, but it is just a party, drinks, dinner, dressing nice. What's not to like?"

He didn't smile back. Instead, he frowned and turned back to his dinner.

What was that about? she thought.

CHAPTER 3

Ethan and Savannah on a walk around the neighborhood later that night

"Savannah?" Ethan turned to her and pulled her to a stop. "Will you be okay around Gregory?"

She glanced over at him. "He hasn't been around for a while."

"Yes, but is that because of the talk you had with him last time he performed at the theatre?"

"We were friends. At least, I thought we were until he overstepped."

"Should I have spoken to him for you?" He didn't like her being alone with that man.

"No, I didn't want to make it more than it was." She shivered a bit when she remembered Gregory's intense stare and his statement of feelings for her.

Ethan saw her shiver and asked, "Are you cold? Should we go in?"

"No, I was just thinking about that night. When I told him

about you, he broke a vase against a wall. He seemed a bit unstable."

"You didn't mention that," Ethan said and gripped her hand tightly.

She grimaced. "Ow, you're hurting me."

"I'm sorry," he said and loosened his grip. "Why didn't you tell me?"

"Because his whole demeanor changed after that and he apologized immediately."

"Has he acted like that before?"

"He's an artist and you know they can be temperamental. But this seemed more than that. I didn't even know he liked me until that night. He'd never asked me out before."

"Would you have gone with him if he asked before we met?"

"No, I don't think so; we didn't have that kind of relationship. At least, I didn't think we did."

"We can send our regrets," he suggested.

"What if this is an olive branch, a way to apologize?"

"It might be," he allowed. "Okay, we can go if your parents don't mind us being away." Her parents had arrived for the wedding and had planned to spend time with them.

"I'll check with them tomorrow. They should be at the theatre."

"We can confirm after you talk to them."

CHAPTER 4

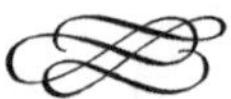

olumbia Theatre the next day

Savannah walked around with her clipboard, monitoring the rehearsal. She wore all black to make herself invisible to the audience from the wings. Stage hands were in place and ready to pull the curtains for the next scene. Others were up in the fly system, adjusting the scenery that needed to be flown in for each scene. She was conducting inventory on the furniture required for each scene. The property master and his crew were assigned to furniture and props, but as stage manager, she liked to do a final check before they were moved onto the stage.

"Savannah."

She turned to the voice and saw her parents standing there. They'd been expected, especially since they had parts in the play currently under rehearsal. Once the play was in good shape and it proved successful, it would be moved to the road for tours throughout the U.S.

"Mom, Dad! Your scenes are coming up," she reminded them as she looked down at her clipboard and checked the call sheet.

"We're going on soon," her dad said, adjusting his tie.

"It's nice to be a supporting character this time," commented her mother as she patted her hair.

"More free time." Her father grinned as walked over to her and leaned in to kiss Savannah's cheek.

Her mother continued. "And I like that we'll be in town for the entire month of December. With the wedding coming up, we want to spend all the time we can with you."

Guilt settled in on Savannah. She pursed her lips and said, "I wanted to talk to you about that."

"Is there something wrong?" her mother asked.

"No, not really. It's just that Ethan and I've been invited to a party a few days before the wedding. I didn't want you to be left on your own."

Her mom looked at her dad before responding. "Well, I think that's taken care of."

"What do you mean?" Savannah asked with a frown.

Her dad pulled out the familiar envelope. "We received this last night."

"You got an invitation? Why?"

"We don't know. We haven't socialized with either of the hosts before. Of course, we know Gregory in passing. We were going to send our regrets. But now that we know you're going, it could be fun."

"It might be. I think this is kind of a business party. We know Gregory from here, and the people at the boarding house work with Geoff. We're all invited."

Such an odd group to have at a party, thought Savannah.

CHAPTER 5

The director called for a lunch break and Savannah grabbed the basket she had asked Amy to put together for her and Ethan. She waved to her parents and walked quickly to Ethan's office.

As she entered the office she found Emma, Ethan, and Mr. Pennington bent over Ethan's desk reviewing a file. She tried to move quietly but Ethan spotted her. "I'll be ready for lunch in just a moment."

"Take your time," she commented. She walked farther across the room and settled against a wall to give them privacy. Ethan worked in a lawyer's office and she understood the need to protect their client's information.

They finished their low conversation with Emma saying, "I'll look into that." She moved toward her office. "Hi, Savannah," she said brightly.

"Hi," Savannah responded.

"Good morning, my dear," Mr. Pennington said. He nodded to Emma and Ethan and headed to his office.

"Sir," she replied and smiled as she watched him close his door.

Ethan walked over to her.

"I hope I didn't interrupt anything."

"You didn't," he assured her. "Lunch?" he then asked hopefully, gesturing to the basket.

"It is." Savannah frowned and looked through the side window by the door. The snow had picked up since she had arrived. "Though I don't think we'll be able to go to the park today."

His gaze followed hers and he nodded. "Maybe here?"

Mr. Pennington provided the solution when he exited the office with his coat and briefcase. "Ethan, I'll be at lunch and then in court this afternoon." He noticed the basket and the weather. "You may take my office for your lunch."

"Thank you, sir," said Ethan

"I'll be back later today," Pennington said. "Emma!"

"Yes, sir, I'm ready." She came into the room quickly with her courier crossbody bag swung over her shoulder. She pulled on her coat and hat and they exited the office together.

Ethan turned to Savannah and picked up the basket with one hand and offered her his other one. She took it and they walked into the office. Once in, he put the basket on the table and she started to take things out of it.

"I talked to my parents about the party. They got an invitation also."

He frowned, "They did?"

"It might have been from Gregory."

"That concerns me even more. What would be the reason?"

"Gregory does know Mom and Dad from the theatre. Maybe this whole thing is for people they both work with?"

Ethan continued to frown. If it was people they worked with, why just Savannah and her parents from the theatre? Savannah was someone Gregory would work with when setting up a show. As the stage manager, they did work together. But her parents were in and out with various shows; they had nothing to do with Gregory except in passing.

"It does make our choice easier. I won't have to worry about not spending time with them. They said they would send in their acceptance."

Ethan shook off the bad feeling. He'd be with her, and what bad things could happen at a party? "Okay, let Emma know we'll be going."

"I will. You know, it could be fun; some rest and relaxation before the wedding."

He smiled. "Yes, a party to remember."

"There's another day I can't wait for," she teased.

"I can't wait for that day," he teased back, knowing she referred to their wedding day.

She smiled back and picked up her sandwich.

CHAPTER 6

J eremy and Emma after dinner that night

Emma pulled back the covers to climb into the bed. "I tried to see Geoff about the party," she commented.

Jeremy paused as he unbuttoned his shirt. "I thought we already told them we were going."

"Yes, Dora sent our RSVP over once Savannah confirmed."

"Then why do you want to talk to him?"

"I'm curious about who he's invited."

Jeremy frowned and sat down on the bed. "We know Dora, Tim, Ethan, Savannah, and us."

"And Savannah's parents," she reminded him. Savannah had mentioned it when she returned from work that evening.

"Is that all you wanted to ask about?" he asked, watching her.

"I'm not sure. I'm just feeling a little off. Why this group? Why now? I went after court today."

"Did you get to see him?" Jeremy's hands tightened for a moment on the shirt he'd taken off.

"No," she said regretfully. "His secretary said he was unavailable."

He forced his hands to relax and asked, "Do you want to send our regrets?"

"No, no. Dora's looking forward to the party. She already has a dress picked out."

"So do you," he reminded her and took off his pants before joining her on the bed.

"So do I," she replied and moved into his arms.

"Then we go?" he asked.

"Then we go," she confirmed.

CHAPTER 7

*W*eekend of December 8th; wedding preparations

Savannah spun, her dress swirling around her. "Oh, Emma, Dora, it's wonderful!"

The dress was white satin and layers of lace flowed down the back and a small bustle. They'd spent every spare moment making the dress. The engagement had happened soon after the sisters' return from Paris a few months before. Emma had worked on the lace while Dora built the satin form.

"Well, hold still," warned Dora, her voice muffled around the needles protruding from between her lips. "I don't want to stick you."

Savannah stopped moving and allowed her to finish working on the hem. Emma walked over to them and attached the final pieces of lace to her bustle. She and Dora both stepped back.

"It's going well; only a few more fittings," Dora said. Emma nodded in agreement. "We need you to take it off. We need to fit the other dress for the party," commented Dora. Emma stepped up to help unlace the back. After the dress was carefully laid on the twin bed, the other dress was taken over to Savannah. This dress was a blue and satin one that Emma had in her closet. Emma needed to add the lace overlay to the sleeves, hem, and scoop neck. As she started to pin it on, the look of the dress changed.

"Oh, Emma, are you sure I can wear this? It's so beautiful," Savannah said, fingering the lace.

"It's perfect for you," Emma assured her.

"But what about you?"

Dora laughed. "We have dresses, the ones we brought from Paris."

"I can't wait to see them on you."

"We can't wait to wear them," Emma commented. Dora laughed.

Savannah fretted, picking at the lace. "I'm not sure I want to go to the party. I just don't think we have time."

Emma removed Savannah's hand and started to attach the lace she had accidentally separated from the garment. She asked casually, "What about the party is bothering you?"

When she didn't answer, Emma asked, "Is there something you want to tell us?"

Savannah sighed. "Gregory got a little forward with me last time we were together."

That comment made Emma start. She looked over at Dora, her eyes wide.

Dora asked, "Does Ethan know?"

"I told him when it happened."

"How does he feel about the party?"

"We were unsure, but my parents are invited. They're excited to attend."

"But they're unaware of what happened between you and Gregory?"

"Yes, we don't want them upset."

"We'll all be there with you," Dora said bracingly.

"Yes, and Ethan will be with me," Savannah said, thinking of him.

This party is going to be interesting, thought Emma.

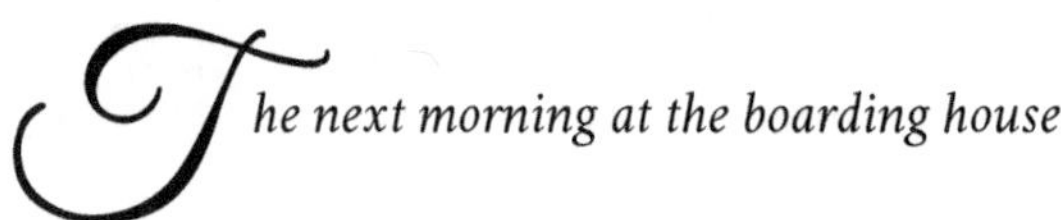

he next morning at the boarding house

"Clair sent a note. She wants you and Jeremy to stop by before work this morning," Tim said as he cut up a piece of toast with jelly on it for three-year-old Lottie. She sat in her chair between Tim and Dora. She grabbed the toast happily as he placed it on her plate.

"Did she say why?" asked Emma, her hand pausing with a fork full of scrambled eggs.

"She just said come by the charity on your way into work."

"I can make the time," Jeremy said. "I can have the carriage arranged."

Emma nodded and finished her food. What could be the reason for Clair's request? Is *there a concern with the charity?* Emma was the head of the board and Clair was the president.

When the meal was finished and plates cleared away, Jeremy and Emma took their lunch kits and moved to the foyer to layer on their winter gear. Emma's bike had been stored in the basement for winter. It would be awhile before it was biking weather again. Winter had set in and walking in the temperatures could be dangerous. Emma pulled on her coat and knit hat before she started to wrap her scarf around her head. She turned and saw a similarly wrapped Jeremy. His voice was muffled when he asked, "Ready?"

She nodded and followed him out to the waiting carriage. The wind blew them back, and Jeremy reached for Emma's hand as they struggled down the stoop. The ride would take about fifteen minutes. The driver jumped down and helped them in. He gave them a heavy blanket and returned to the driver's seat on the top of the carriage.

The trip took longer than normal due to the snow and wind. Once there, Jeremy helped Emma down and he paid the driver. The driver waved, happy to be returning to a warm shelter.

They entered the building that housed the charity they were on the board for. The accounting offices for Geoff were also in the building. At the time the charity was formed, it made sense to have them in the same place. The building was six stories. Geoff had taken the fourth floor for his business and the 6th as his apartment.

The charity was on the second floor and, more than anything, she wanted to tell the elevator operator to go to the fourth floor. She took a deep breath and reminded herself why they were at the building. The doors opened to their floor and they headed to the solid wood doors of the business. Jeremy tried the door and it opened easily. They stepped inside the large room and saw Lily Edwards already at her desk.

"Jeremy, Emma, we're glad you could be here this morning," Lily greeted them. "I'll let Clair know you're here." Emma and Jeremy removed their coats, scarves, and hats as they waited. When Lily returned, she took their coats and other winter gear. "Go on in, she's waiting for you."

They walked quickly to Clair's office. It was a large room,

done with dark browns and blues as the primary colors. Clair stood as they entered and walked around her desk. Even at 9:00 in the morning, she was beautifully dressed in purple and her hair was coiffed.

She greeted them warmly. "Thank you for coming in this morning, it's important." She moved to the door and called out, "Lily, could you join us?"

Lily entered and Clair asked everyone to sit at the long table that was on the opposite side of the room from them.

"Are you sure you need me?" Lily asked. She stayed near the door.

"Yes, we need to talk about Henrietta."

She nodded and walked to the long table. They sat and Emma asked, "Henrietta?"

"Is she okay?" Jeremy asked.

"We've been sending Henrietta to school at the Rutherford Academy, then she'd work here most weekdays," Clair reminded them.

"Is there a problem with her work?" Jeremy frowned. He and Emma had been busy this year with cases and the trip to Paris. *Has it been too long since we checked in with her?*

Emma took his hand. Jeremy had taken an interest in the girl when he'd investigated a glass factory that primarily hired children to work. He'd improved conditions there, but the children were all still under their employ. That was all, except for Henrietta. They'd offered to pay for school and gave her a job at the charity. Her parents hadn't shown much interest in her except for a paycheck.

"No, she's very smart and was helping out with our various projects. It isn't that. It's because she suddenly stopped showing up. I followed up with her school and they said the same thing."

"When?" Jeremy asked.

"A few weeks ago."

"Why weren't we notified sooner? What if something's happened to her?" Jeremy asked worriedly.

"It hasn't," Lily assured him.

Emma turned to her. "How do you know?"

"I went to Henrietta's home and waited for her to leave and I followed her. She went to a sewing factory and she appears to work there."

"How long was she there?"

"I left and went back that evening; she didn't leave until late."

"How is this happening?" Jeremy stood quickly, his chair falling behind him. He pushed back his brown curls with his hand. He saw it shaking and stopped himself.

Emma saw how this information was affecting him and asked, "What can we do?"

"Not a lot if her parents have made this decision," Clair stated. Kids belonged to their parents and they had the final say on any and everything pertaining to their children.

"Well, it's a bad decision," he muttered.

"Yes," Emma agreed, "why don't we go over there and find out what's changed?"

"I think that would be for the best," Clair said. "I've spoken to her teachers and she has time to catch up if she comes back soon."

"If you get her back, I can help with that," Lily said.

"We all can," said Emma firmly. "Jeremy?"

"This evening?" He wanted to go over there now and get answers.

"We'll want both parents present for this conversation."

"All right." He sighed. He hated to think of Henrietta anywhere that wasn't safe.

"After the bakery?" she asked. Emma worked at the family bakery in the evenings during the holiday season.

"Okay, I'll meet you there." He turned to Clair. "Henrietta will be back in school tomorrow."

"And we look forward to seeing her back here," she replied.

Emma and Jeremy hugged Clair and Lily and then headed out and down the elevator. The day would be a long wait until they could find out why Henrietta had been removed from school.

CHAPTER 9

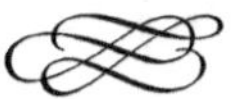

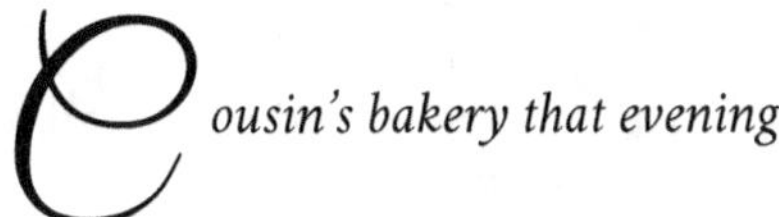 *ousin's bakery that evening*

The bakery door opened and cold air hit Emma's face. "Door!" everyone called. The door closed and Emma continued to move her cookies to the gift boxes. She felt lips on her neck and she leaned back. "Better not let my companion catch you doing that," she giggled. "He's the jealous type."

"Ha ha," Jeremy said. "About ready to go?" He was eager to get moving. It was late and already dark.

"Just about; help me finish."

He moved beside her and helped place the rest of the cookies and pastries into the boxes at her work station. He noticed a basket. "Who's that for?"

"For the Lawsons, Henrietta's parents."

Jeremy raised his eyebrows.

"I was hoping we could begin on friendly terms."

"Yeah, bribery's always good. It's probably better than my plan."

"Which is?" Though she could probably guess.

"Yelling, screaming, threatening to tear them limb from limb. That kind of thing. Oh, and demanding to know why they pulled her out of school."

"Is it possible this was Henrietta's idea?" Emma knew the girl could be stubborn about how she wanted things to work.

"No, you saw how she sparkled when school was mentioned. Clair said she loved it."

"Until lately."

"Yeah, I wish we'd paid more attention to what was going on with her."

She didn't respond to that statement. Instead, she called out, "Cousin! I'm finished with my boxes, and they're marked with what's in them."

Cousin looked up from the list he was carrying. "Danke. Same time tomorrow?"

"Yes, I'll be here. Let me grab my coat." She went to the closet, took off her apron, and replaced it with her coat, hat, scarf, and gloves. She exited and found Jeremy had bundled up.

"The carriage is waiting outside." He carried the basket out as they quickly approached the carriage and climbed in. The driver knew the address and started them off toward Henrietta's house.

"How do we do this?" she asked.

"Hear them out calmly and rationally… at least at first."

"And if we don't like what we hear?"

"We offer alternatives." He already had one in his pocket. The conversation would go his way.

They went quiet, thinking about that as they made their way through the snow.

Once at Lawson's house, Jeremy paid the driver and helped Emma down. He called up, "Come back in an hour; we'll meet you here."

"I'll be here," the driver said. "Now, for somewhere warm."

He shivered and got the horse moving with a click of his tongue.

Jeremy took the basket and held out his hand to Emma; she took it and they went up to the small house. He knocked and the door swung open.

"What do you want?" Henrietta's mom asked belligerently.

Jeremy unwrapped his scarf and she recognized him immediately and started to close the door on them. He stopped her with his hand and asked with a harsh tone, "Can we come in?"

Mrs. Lawson stood in the doorway, not moving, blocking their entry. "Let 'em in," called a deep voice from inside the room. She moved back stiffly. "Sit," that deep voice directed from the corner.

Jeremy and Emma walked to the wooded chairs set up in the small room. She sat the basket next to them and they looked at the large man.

"I'm Henrietta's father," he said.

Jeremy started. "We're here about her. She hasn't been in school or her afternoon job."

Mrs. Lawson jumped into the conversation. "Ain't none of your business? She's our flesh and blood. Not yours!"

Emma started to balk at the possessive voice; Jeremy pressed firmly on her hand. "But…" she started.

Jeremy shook his head and turned back to the Lawsons. "How much?"

Emma's eyes widened but she didn't say anything.

Lawson took over the conversation from there. He looked at his wife. "I told you." He laughed cruelly. He looked back to Jeremy and rubbed his hands together. "I want enough to leave town with my wife and start somewhere else."

"You know this'll be a one-time payment only," Jeremy said, "and we expect you to have no contact whatsoever with Henrietta after this."

The wife stuttered, trying to make an argument. Lawson

turned his head her way, scowling. She shrunk back. "Fine, you handle it," she said meekly.

The two men hammered out the deal. It could have been a product being bought and sold instead of the livelihood of a young girl with numbers being negotiated and settled upon.

"Do you need my notebook?" Emma asked.

"No," Jeremy responded, pulling a folded piece of paper from his pocket. He'd planned for this and had already filled out the numbers.

"Sign here," he said and signed his name under Lawson's. He pulled out his wallet and handed over the money. "Now, where can we find her?" he asked as he took the paper and folded it.

"She's at Tummons on 15th."

Jeremy frowned but didn't comment; that was one of the worst locations for workers in the city. They'd been fined multiple times for locking the workers inside the facility.

"Emma, let's go. We need to pick up Henrietta."

They started out and Emma retrieved her basket. She was damned if she was going to leave it with them. The allotted time had passed and the carriage was waiting for them.

"Take us to Tummons on 15th," called Jeremy.

The driver nodded and, once they were on their way, Emma looked over at him. "You knew before we came here that you'd need to buy Henrietta from them."

"I did. I know those kinds of people. Money's the only reason they still have anything to do with Henrietta."

Emma pondered, "Were they a family before Aiden died?" Aiden was Henrietta's brother who had worked and died in the glass factory.

"Probably not. You know how families like that are. The focus was just on the boy's in the family. Did you see his pictures on the mantel? His ball and glove?"

"There were no photos of Henrietta."

"She seems like an afterthought."

"Unfortunately, it's the boys who get all the love and attention in families like that. Girls aren't good for anything except when it comes to the money."

"Sad."

They pulled to a stop and Jeremy climbed down to help her. When they started to go in, Emma stopped him and requested, "Let me do this. I'll tell them it's an emergency."

"That would probably be for the best. I'll wait here."

Emma hurried up the stairs of the warehouse and pounded on the door. It opened slowly, and a large woman stood there. "What is it?"

"I need Henrietta Lawson; it's an emergency."

"After her shift," the woman said and started to close the door. When it wouldn't close, she looked down and saw Emma's foot in the door. She also saw the knife Emma held in her hand.

"You know I'm pretty good with knives," Emma said as she turned the blade slowly in her hand.

The woman watched the knife and swung the door open. "I don't want any trouble. She's in the main room that way." She pointed down the hallway.

Emma stowed her knife and ran to the room where she could hear machines running. As she entered, she called, "Henrietta! Henrietta Lawson!"

"Emma?" came a small voice. "You're here?"

Emma looked around but couldn't see the girl, "Henrietta, come toward me."

A small girl stepped out into the walkway from between the running machines. It was Henrietta and she had a black eye. Emma held out her arms and Henrietta ran into them. She lifted her up and moved toward the exit.

"She won't get paid if she leaves," the woman called out as Emma carried Henrietta out.

"She won't need it," Emma said over her shoulder. She set Henrietta down, took off her coat and hat, and wrapped the girl up. She picked her back up and made her way to the carriage. Jeremy jumped down to help them in.

"Home," called Jeremy. The driver immediately started out.

Emma held Henrietta to her; Jeremy took off his coat and laid it on them. Emma mouthed, *Thanks*.

He didn't answer; he leaned into them to offer more warmth.

At the boarding house, she handed down Henrietta to Jeremy. They ran quickly up the steps and into the house.

Dora came in to welcome them. "Dinner just started." She stopped suddenly when she saw they had a child with them. "Who do we have here?" Jeremy sat Henrietta down and Emma unwrapped her.

"This is Henrietta," Emma told her sister.

The little girl smiled, then grimaced and gingerly touched her eye.

Dora immediately went into mothering mode. "Let's go get a cool rag for that." As she led Henrietta to the kitchen, Jeremy and Emma hung their coats in the closet. Jeremy looked over at Emma. "Did we just become parents?" he asked.

Emma grabbed the table to steady herself. "Wow, I think we just did."

"Are you okay?" he asked, hiding a smile.

"Yes, I think I am. We can do this." She held out her hand to him and he took it. "We can do this together." He nodded and they went into the dining room.

Dora and Henrietta were coming out of the kitchen, with Henrietta holding a wet cloth to her face. When she saw Lottie, she immediately went over to the little girl. She put down her wet cloth and picked up the baby. Henrietta swirled Lottie around and the people around the table laughed. "Not too much," cautioned Dora. "She might get sick."

She put Lottie back in her chair. "I just love babies," she said.

"Well, you'll get plenty of time to play with her. Now, sit down and eat," Jeremy said.

Dora looked at Tim, her eyebrows raised. He shrugged.

Emma picked up the wet rag, handed it to Henrietta, and pointed out a chair next to her. She sat. "Everyone, this is Henrietta."

"Hen, Hen, Hen!" shouted Lottie.

"I like that," said Henrietta.

"Welcome," came from all sides of the table. Platters started to be passed around and the family filled their plates. After dinner, the children—Lottie, Henrietta, and Patrick—moved into the sitting room. The rest of the family helped clear the table and clean up.

"What're your plans for Henrietta?" Dora asked Emma.

Emma continued to dry the plate she held and glanced over at her sister. "Henrietta is going to live here with us."

"And just who'll be her parent?" Dora asked. She and Tim already had two children and several successful businesses. She hadn't planned on a third child.

Jeremy took Emma's hand and said, "We will."

"You know that means making arrangements for her when you're on cases that take you out of town."

Tim turned off the water and said, "We'll help, but we'll need notice."

Dora nodded. "Yes, that's right." There needed to be a clear line on who would manage her care.

Once everything was clean and put away, Amy waved on her way out the kitchen door. Ethyl and Jake accompanied her out. Jake would walk Ethyl home and then return to the boarding house.

The group moved into the dining room. They stopped in the doorway and looked at the children. Patrick was reading a book while Hen was lying on her back and lifting Lottie in the air. The little girl was giggling in delight.

"I think Hen is going to be spending a lot of time with Lottie," Emma commented.

"She does seem to be enjoying herself. Will she be in school?" asked Dora.

Jeremy said, "She goes to a private school and then works with Clair in the afternoons."

"Is that too much for her?"

"I think she needs her schedule to keep her busy and out of trouble," said Jeremy, thinking about the case she'd been involved in.

"We'll work through that as we go," Emma said. "There'll be vacation days we'll have to think about."

"She'll need a bedroom," commented Tim.

Dora considered that. "We have several on the third floor." She looked over at Emma and asked, "Come up with me?"

Emma took her arm and they walked up together to examine one of the unoccupied rooms. Once inside, Emma flopped down on the bed.

"You made a major decision very quickly. Was it the right one?" her sister asked, crossing her arms.

"Yes," she said, raising herself up on her elbows. "And I know Jeremy wants this. She's an amazing girl, so smart."

"Jeremy mentioned trouble?" Dora relaxed her arms and sat next to Emma on the bed.

"No, trouble isn't right. She's a good child; she just has a fierce sense of right and wrong. We have to figure out a way to channel that into something positive. You know, she's so smart, I think she can go to college."

"Wow! Really?" Dora knew that not many women were able to gain acceptance into college.

"She's that smart."

Dora pushed off the bed, stood, and moved around the room. "I'll get the clean sheets." She walked out of the room and came back with fresh sheets and towels. The room was ready for a boarder, but they were picky about who lived with them. The space had been open for a while.

They stripped the sheets and added new ones. "I didn't notice she carried any bags with her," Dora commented.

"Yeah, we'll go back tomorrow to get her things."

Dora didn't ask for details, but instead said, "We can loan her a nightshirt and a dress for tomorrow. I think we have some from when we were her age."

Emma went back downstairs with Dora. Everyone had moved to the sitting room; Lottie played with Henrietta and Patrick had settled into a card game with his dad and Jeremy.

Emma walked over to where Henrietta sat on the floor and asked, "Would you like to see your room?"

"Yes, please," she said and took Lottie to her dad.

Jeremy started to stand to accompany them.

"I can take care of it," Emma said and waved him back.

Jeremy smiled slightly, holding his cards loosely in his hands.

"I can see your cards, Uncle Jeremy," Patrick scolded.

"Oh, of course, what was I thinking?" asked Jeremy, giving Tim a wink.

Emma and Henrietta ascended the stairs. "Will I really have my own room?" the girl asked. She'd never had her own before. Aiden had gotten the second bedroom and she'd slept in the living room. Even after he died, she'd continued to stay in the living room.

"Yes, all your own."

"Where's your room?"

"On the second floor." Emma pointed it out on their way to the third floor. "You can come to me if you ever need anything, just be sure to knock first." She'd have to make sure her door stayed locked at night. She and Jeremy had an adjoining room and he spent the nights with her.

"All right."

Once they reached the next floor, they went to the first room. At the door, Emma said, "You can go in."

Henrietta still hesitated but finally pushed the door open. It was a nice size bedroom with a bed, desk dresser, and a fireplace. Henrietta walked to the center of the room and turned slowly in a circle. "It's mine and I don't have to share?"

"All yours, and no, you won't have to share," Emma confirmed.

Henrietta started to cry.

Emma walked over quickly, alarmed at the mood change. "Hen, what is it?"

"I'm so happy. I just wish Aiden could be here with us."

Emma wrapped the girl in a hug. She pulled back after a long moment. "Would you like to get ready for bed?"

"I don't have anything with me."

A knock sounded at the door. "Come in," Emma called.

It was Dora. "I have your nightclothes and toothbrush," she told Henrietta.

Henrietta took them and looked like she might cry again. "Thank you, Dora."

She leaned down and kissed Henrietta on the cheek. "We're glad you're with us." And with that, Dora left.

"Let me show you the bathroom," Emma commented.

Henrietta followed and looked at the bathroom in awe. They didn't have an indoor water closet at her home. Emma realized she needed to show her how to use the facilities. "Once you're done dressing, go back to your room. Call down the stairs and I'll come up and say good night." Henrietta nodded and continued to look around the room.

Emma walked downstairs and into the sitting room. Jeremy sat reading by himself. "What happened to everyone?" she asked, sitting next to him on the settee.

"Bedtime." His mouth quirked. "Did you get Hen settled?"

"Yes, we have a lot to learn."

"Come here," he said and put his book down. She relaxed into his arms and laid her head on his chest. "We'll need to be there for her and have limits for her to adhere to."

"Yes."

"And we need to go by her old home and get her things."

"Yes. Early tomorrow?"

"Sure."

"Emma," called a small voice down the stairs.

"I think that's for you," he said.

"I think so, too." Emma stood and walked to the door.

"Hang on, I'll walk up with you," called Jeremy.

"That would be nice," she said and waited for him to join her. They held hands and walked up together. On the third floor, they found Hen in her borrowed nightshirt standing by her door.

"Jeremy, hi," she said.

"Hi, Henrietta. Do you like your room?"

"I love it." She looked over at Emma. "She said I can stay here with you and the rest of the family."

"Yes, we want you as part of our family." She ran to him and he hugged her tightly.

Emma wiped away a tear and said, "Okay, it's time for bed. You have school tomorrow and you have two weeks to catch up."

Henrietta smiled. She didn't mind; she loved school.

"Bed now," said Emma. They followed her in and watched her climb into her bed. Emma pulled up the covers to tuck her in. "Breakfast in the dining room in the morning."

"Oh no!" Henrietta exclaimed.

"What's wrong?" Jeremy asked.

"My dress is dirty! I didn't wash it out."

"I will take care of that, but for tomorrow, there's a dress hanging in the closet over there." She indicated it with her hand.

"It was one of mine from when I was your age. You can wear that."

Hen nodded and settled down on the bed.

Emma leaned down and kissed her cheek. "Now sleep. You know where my room is if you need anything."

Henrietta nodded. "Good night."

"Good night," Emma and Jeremy commented as they turned down the light and left the room. Quietly, they headed to their individual rooms and got ready for bed. Emma was in bed reading when Jeremy came through the bookcase door. He ran over and jumped on the bed.

"I'm enjoying being in the same place as you."

"Paris was fun," she said contemplatively.

"Yes, and it's somewhere I want us to return to."

"That would be wonderful. We'll go when the time is right."

"Yes."

CHAPTER 10

"It's time to get up," Jeremy said, poking Emma.

"Ummph. 'S too early," Emma moaned and burrowed further into the bed.

He pulled back the cover. "It's Henrietta's first day back at school."

Emma opened her eyes and found he was already dressed. "Am I late?" she asked, sitting up quickly and pushing her hair back off her face.

"No. But I'm nervous about our first day as Henrietta's guardians. I just don't want to get it wrong."

"You won't. We just need to be on the same page and love her."

"Yes. Get dressed."

She got up, hurried to the bathroom to wash up, then returned to her bedroom to dress. *It's going to be a day of new experiences,* she thought as she pulled her hair into a bun and pulled her laces tight on her boots. It was still cold, so she pulled on a sweater.

Jeremy had waited for her; he put down his book and said, "See you on the other side." He went through his bookcase and, when she opened her door into the hallway, he exited at the same time.

"How did you do that?" Hen asked from the stairs. She'd seen them leave their rooms.

"Do what?" asked Jeremy innocently.

"You came out at the same time."

"Did we?" murmured Emma. *Big eyes,* she thought.

"Must be magic," Jeremy said.

Emma looked the girl over and saw her old dress fit her well. "You look very nice."

"You do," agreed Jeremy.

"I love it, thank you," Henrietta said, moving her hand over her skirt. "I won't get it dirty," she promised.

Emma bent down to be eye-to-eye with her. "You can get it dirty; it's yours now."

"It is! Thank you."

"Anyone ready for breakfast?" Jeremy asked the two of them.

Both nodded and they walked down together and went into the dining room. The food was set up and Jake sat at the far end of the table reading a photography book.

They sat and Henrietta started to reach for the food closest to her. "Let's wait for everyone to sit down," Emma said.

She put down her hands and nodded.

It wasn't long before the rest of the family joined them. Lottie shrieked, "Hen! Hen!" Henrietta waved at her, but she was more interested in breakfast. Once everyone sat, the food started to be passed around. Henrietta piled as much as she could on her plate. Dora came over. "Here let me help with this. How about a little bit of everything?" She gave her a more moderate portion of eggs, bacon, toast, and fruit.

Henrietta nodded and said, "Thank you."

Dora kissed her on the head and moved back to her chair. Lottie had finished her breakfast and was talking happily. Dora set up her plate and ate her breakfast.

As they finished, Emma turned to Henrietta. "Are you ready to go to school?"

"Yes," Henrietta said eagerly and stood. At that moment, six biscuits fell from Henrietta's lap onto the floor. She scrambled to pick them up.

Jeremy knelt next to her and said, "You can take these with you or we can keep them here for you."

"They'll be here when I get back? No one will take them?" Henrietta asked, clearly torn at leaving the food behind.

"No one takes them," assured Emma, kneeling next to them. "They'll still be here. Why don't you give them to me and I'll make sure they're put somewhere safe until you get home."

"Home?" asked Henrietta.

"Yes. Home," Jeremy and Emma said at the same time.

Henrietta grinned and handed over the biscuits. Emma placed them on the table and wrapped a clean napkin around them.

"I'll take that to the kitchen," Dora said and walked over to take them from Emma. "They'll be here when you get home," she promised the girl.

"Thank you."

They moved to the foyer. Dora ran out to them with their lunches. "Don't forget these," she said and handed each their lunch.

"Thanks, Dora. I was a little distracted," said Emma.

She kissed her sister on the cheek. "I understand."

Emma walked to the closet and pulled out three coats. She handed Jeremy his and held one up for Henrietta.

"Mama's coat," murmured Dora.

"Yes, I thought she could use it until we get her own."

"It might be a little large," said Dora, "but I think it will be perfect."

Emma and Henrietta pulled on their coats. Dora helped Henrietta roll up her sleeves.

"There are extra hats and gloves in the drawer there," said Dora.

Jeremy went over and pulled them out. He tossed them to Henrietta to put on.

Once all were dressed for the wintery weather, they walked to the door.

Dora called to them, "What time will everyone be home?"

Emma turned back. "Henrietta will go to Clair's after school and I'll pick her up from there on the way home from the bakery."

Dora nodded and watched them leave. Tim walked up behind her and put his arms around her waist. "Did they make it out?"

"Yes."

"What was up with the biscuits?"

"I think Henrietta's trying to save food for when she might not have any."

He squeezed her in reaction to the comment. "They starved her?"

"There might not have been enough to go around and growing girls are usually hungry."

"Will you save them for her?"

"Of course, we want her to trust us. We need to show her that there will always be food when she's hungry."

CHAPTER 11

A carriage stood outside and Hen asked in a muffled voice, "Aren't we walking to school?"

"Not in this weather," commented Jeremy,

He helped Emma and Henrietta into the carriage. Once they were in and the driver pulled away, Jeremy pulled down his scarf and asked Henrietta, "Do you like school?"

"I do," she said through the scarf, then moved it down to repeat, "I do. I've missed it."

"Well, you get to go back," he said. "Will you be able to catch up on the last two weeks?"

"I'll be able to," she said confidently.

"We can help," said Emma. "Lily also said she'd help."

"And Christmas break is coming up," Henrietta said.

So many things are coming up: Hen's vacation, that party, and the wedding, thought Emma.

They sat back and watched the snow fall outside the carriage. The school appeared in the distance. "Get ready," Emma told Henrietta. "We'll be stopping soon." They pulled up and Jeremy descended to the ground. He paid the driver and then called for Emma and Henrietta to step down. He lifted them out, one at a time, to the ground.

"Come back for us in about 30 minutes," he call to the driver. He turned to them, grabbed their hand and said, "Let's go." They navigated the snow-filled ground and climbed the steps, watching for ice. They made it to the top, he pushed the door open, and they went in. Once inside, Emma helped him push the door closed against the icy wind.

"Can I help you?" a voice called from down the hall.

They unwrapped their scarves and removed their hats. "Henrietta!" called the same voice. A woman ran over to her and hugged her. "Are you back with us?"

Jeremy answered for her. "She is. We'll need to speak with the principal."

"Of course," she said. "I'm Ada Nelson, the office manager."

"I'm Jeremy Tilden and this is Emma Evans."

"How about I get Henrietta to her class? And then I'll get you to the principal," said Ada.

"Can we accompany her to the class?" Emma asked. She was hoping to observe Henrietta in that environment. Is *she happy here?*

"Of course, follow me." They walked with the office manager to the class. Henrietta seemed at ease and talked all the way to the classroom. The school day hadn't started and students were standing around talking. When Henrietta entered, the students called her name and waved her over. She grinned and turned to Emma and Jeremy. "Do I go to the foundation after school?"

It was nearby but might be dangerous in the current weather. "Yes," said Jeremy, "I'll have someone here to take you over."

The girl nodded and ran off to join her friends.

Henrietta's teacher walked over and said, "I don't think we've met. Are you Henrietta's parents?"

"No, but we're her guardians," Emma said. "Her parents will be leaving the area soon and Henrietta will be staying with us."

His eyebrows rose but he nodded. His only concern was Henrietta's education. "She's a few weeks behind on her studies."

Emma asked, "Can you compile what she needs to catch up on and we can help her with it?"

"I have no doubt." He chuckled. "She was already ahead when she disappeared. I'll send it home with her."

"Good," Jeremy said as the students started to take their seats.

Ada said, "Class will be starting soon." Jeremy and Emma nodded and followed her out.

They went back the same way they'd come but stopped at a door. Ada pushed it open to reveal an office. "Mr. Higginbotham is in his office. I'll see if he has time for you." She walked to a door on the far wall.

While they waited, Emma whispered, "What do we tell him?"

"The truth. We're now her guardians." He pulled out the signed paper. "I have this if there are any questions."

She nodded and they waited where they were. A few moments later, Ada returned, "You can go in."

Emma and Jeremy followed her direction and entered the office. The man they were there to see sat at a large desk with bookshelves lined up behind him. He immediately stood, walked over to them, and made introductions.

"Hello, I'm James Higginbotham. I understand you brought Henrietta back to school. I'm so happy to hear that."

The man seemed sincere and Emma liked what she'd seen of the school.

"We wanted to talk to you," Jeremy started. "We've taken Henrietta into our home and we're now her guardians."

"Hmm." Higginbotham walked to his desk and sat down behind it. "Have a seat, please."

They sat.

"Do you have some paperwork for me to review on the guardianship?"

"I do." Jeremy pulled it out and handed it to him.

Higginbotham reviewed it. "It looks to be in order," he said. "I have to be honest, I'm relieved this has occurred." Emma frowned as he continued. "I've been to Henrietta's home and met her parents."

"When was this?" Emma asked.

"A few weeks ago, when she first stopped coming to school."

"Do you take such an interest in all of your students?" asked Jeremy.

"I do, especially when they're at the top of their class and then disappear with no explanation. We were all concerned. I was not happy with the response I got from Mr. and Mrs. Lawson when I stressed how important her schooling was."

"Yes, they didn't appreciate the value of education."

"That's an understatement. They were verbally abusive and seemed to only have her to provide a paycheck."

Emma and Jeremy nodded. "You saw what we did," Emma responded.

Higginbotham held up the document and said, "I won't ask how this was achieved. I'm happy with the final results."

Jeremy nodded and didn't comment.

The principal gave him a long look before handing it back to him. "I hope we'll see Henrietta on a more routine basis now."

"You can count on it," said Emma. "Education will provide her with a path forward."

He smiled suddenly. "I'll expect to see you at the parent-teacher nights," he said.

"We'll be there," said Jeremy. Emma nodded her agreement.

Higginbotham sat back. "You know, it's funny."

"What's that?" asked Jeremy.

"We had someone else asking about Henrietta."

"When was this?" Emma asked, sitting forward on her chair.

"It was before she left school."

Emma's eyes narrowed. "What were the questions?"

"This person wanted her address and the names of her parents."

"Why?" Jeremy asked.

"They spoke to Ada. You might ask her."

"We will," Jeremy said.

"Then I think that's all we need. If you'll get with Ada, she'll update the contact information in the files."

They stood. Emma and Jeremy shook hands with him. "Thank you."

"No," Higginbotham said, "thank you for getting Henrietta back to us."

They left the office and Ada pulled out the necessary paperwork. They completed it and Emma asked, "The person who was inquiring about Henrietta, did you get a name?"

"No, I'm afraid not. He didn't want to leave one."

"Did he say why he wanted the information?" asked Jeremy.

"No, I asked but he cut me off."

"What did he look like?"

"He never took off his hat or scarf and I didn't see his hair. He was a few inches shorter than you," Ada replied, looking at Jeremy.

"Thank you for not giving out any information. We appreciate your protecting her," Jeremy told her.

"We do that for all of our students," she assured them.

"Thank you again."

They stepped outside and Emma turned to Jeremy. "Is someone after Henrietta? Is she in some kind of danger?"

"We'll protect her."

Jeremy hailed his carriage and Emma said, "I'll stop by Clair's and pick up Hen on the way home."

He leaned over and kissed her. "Let me know if anything

changes. I'll make sure she's picked up and moved after school." The carriage pulled up and he lifted her in. "Do you have time to go to Henrietta's home with me?" he asked, leaning in.

"I think so; it should be fine," said Emma, drumming her fingers on her lips.

"What're you planning?" asked Jeremy. He knew when Emma drummed her fingers on her lips that she was making plans.

"Hm? Just thinking for now. We can use the cold as a reason for getting Henrietta to and from school and Clair's."

"Yes." He stepped back and called up the new address to the driver. He climbed in and pulled her close to him. The trip to the Lawson's house took a while with the weather and the distance. The longer it took, the more agitated Jeremy got.

"What is it?" she asked him.

"The distance. She had to walk all the way to the school and back each day."

"Yes."

"We set up the schooling but we didn't provide her safe transport? She could have gotten taken at any time and we weren't even aware of it." Their previous cases had involved kids being taken from families too easily because they were left alone for long periods.

"We'll take care and make sure she's safe now," she reassured him, taking his hand.

He continued to grasp it until they stopped.

"Are you ready?" he asked.

"I am," she said and opened the door. He jumped down and turned to help her out.

"Come back for us in about twenty minutes," he called to the driver.

They walked toward the small home and knocked on the door. It swung open. Jeremy looked at her questioningly. "I guess we go in?"

"Let's go," she said gratefully. The wind had picked up again.

Once inside, the wind had cut back but not the temperature. It was the same as outside and there was no heat in the space. They looked around. There was no furniture or other belongings. All signs of life in the place were gone.

"They've left," Emma stated.

"Seems that way," said Jeremy as he strode to the two side rooms. He returned quickly. "Everything's gone."

"They took everything and left nothing for Henrietta?" she asked in disbelief.

"Looks like. It won't matter anyway; we'll provide her what she needs."

Emma kicked some scraps of paper she saw on the floor. "It just makes me sad."

"I agree, but think positively; they're gone."

"I wish they…" She didn't finish what she was saying and bent down to turn over one of the scraps.

"You were saying?" he asked.

"What?" she asked, distracted. "Oh, yay!"

"What is it?" he asked curiously and walked over to her.

It was a small picture. "I think it might be Henrietta and Aiden."

The picture was small and crinkled. "I think you're right. We can take it and have it framed for her."

"Why would they take her things?" Emma asked, exasperated.

"I'm not sure she had any. I only ever saw her in the one dress."

"That's true." Emma still felt a bit sad, thinking of the keepsakes she had from both her mama and papa.

"Come on, let's start our day," said Jeremy.

They exited and found their carriage waiting.

They climbed back into it and made their way to her office first. At the office door, she waved to Jeremy and went in. She grasped the door firmly because the wind was whipping. Ethan ran over and helped her close it.

"You're a bit late this morning," he commented.

"Whew!" she said and removed her scarf and hat. "Yes, we had to take Henrietta to school."

"Any concerns? Mr. Pennington put together the paperwork for the guardianship for Jeremy. He said I could help if needed." Jeremy had sent over a note to update Mr. Pennington on the outcome.

"No, thank goodness. The document he provided makes it clear we're Henrietta's guardians. The school accepted it with no questions."

"Good. Your files are on my desk."

"Thanks," she said, pulling off her coat and moving it to the closet. She took the files and settled into her office.

CHAPTER 12

The day went by quickly for Emma; there were several cases that required her to research. She cleaned off her desk and headed to the outer office. Ethan's face was buried in a file.

"Hey, I'm leaving."

"Okay," he said, not looking up.

She got her coat and headed to her late afternoon job at the bakery. While she boxed up her order, her mind was on where she was going next—to Henrietta. On her way out, she called goodbye and exited through the front. Carriages were lined up for business; she hailed one and asked the driver to take her to the foundation. He jumped down and helped her into the carriage. The door closed and she shivered, folding her arms to her chest and burrowing down in her scarf. It wasn't long until they pulled to a stop. When he helped her out, she asked, "Can you stay? I'll be coming out with a child."

"It'll be extra and this trip up is to be paid now."

"Of course." She handed him the money and a tip to wait. She hurried into the multi-storied building; the security officer on the first floor waved her way through. The foundation she led owned the building. The elevator operator held the door for her, and she told him the floor she needed and stepped further into the car. Geoff's floor number passed by; she'd been distracted by Hen, but now she remembered the party.

It's just a party, she chided herself. *Why berate the man over the invite?*

The doors slid open and she walked to the double doors and into Lily's office. Lily sat at the desk. "Good afternoon, Emma," she greeted.

"Hi, I'm here to pick up Henrietta. Where is she?" Emma asked, looking around.

"She's in the office with Clair; they're working on the invitations for the next gala."

"Can I go in?"

"Sure. Hey, Emma."

"Yes?"

"We're glad she's back. She was missed."

"That's nice to hear," Emma replied, smiling. She opened Clair's door and found Henrietta at a small table sitting beside Clair's desk, working on addressing envelopes.

Clair was at her desk and stood as soon as she saw her. Her dress rustled as she made her way over. They hugged. "You're doing a good thing," Clair murmured in Emma's ear before straightening.

Emma nodded and looked toward Henrietta. "Ready to head home?"

"Yes!" She put her work into a pile and turned to Clair. "I can work on this tomorrow."

"There's no rush. We won't send them out until next year," Clair assured the girl.

Henrietta walked to Emma and put her arm around her waist. Emma smiled and put her arm around her shoulder. "Do you have your homework?"

"Oops," she said and broke away to run back to the table.

"Do you have a lot of homework?"

"Some. Lily helped me get a bit done earlier and I should be able to finish before the Christmas holidays."

"Why don't you go say goodbye to Lily?" suggested Clair.

"Okay," the girl said brightly and left the office.

Clair looked at Emma. "Are you a mama now?"

Emma shrugged. "More of a close friend."

"Remember, friend, kids need limits," Clair cautioned her.

"I'll have to work on that," Emma said wryly. "Were you invited to Geoff's Christmas party?"

"I was not."

"Why not?" Emma asked, ready to be outraged for her. "Was it because…"

"Of my past?" she filled in. Clair had been a madam when they first met. She was a very successful businesswoman who had changed her life and took on the job of managing the foundation when asked by Emma. "No, it isn't that. It's never come up or been an issue. I'm not sure what the agenda is for that party, but the group he has invited is quite small."

"How do you know who's been invited?" asked Emma curiously.

"Lily and his secretary talk."

"Oh. Tell me who's on the list."

"Let me see," Clair said. "There's you and Jeremy, Dora, Tim, Ethan, Savannah. Oh, and Savannah's parents."

Emma moved to perch on the edge of the desk. "I found the invite to Savannah's parents off. Why invite them?"

"Nathan, his secretary, told Lily it was so that her parents wouldn't be left alone the night of the party."

"I guess that's nice of him. We've never socialized with Geoff before this," said Emma. "Je keeps his distance from us."

"He donates to the foundation, though."

"Yes, but he never attends any functions."

"That's true. I've invited him to all of them."

"Then why now? And this group of people?"

"I had the same concerns," Clair started.

Henrietta came back into the room. "Emma! The carriage driver sent word up that we need to get going!"

Emma looked at Clair. "Talk later?"

"Of course."

Emma turned to Hen and said, "I'm ready. Let's go." She looked over to Clair and mouthed, *Thank you.*

Clair smiled and said to Henrietta, "I'll see you tomorrow."

"I'll be here," the girl promised.

Lily had noticed they were keeping a close eye on Henrietta's movements. She walked over to Emma and said, " Geoff's secretary inquired about Henrietta's school. I told him, because I was so proud of how she was doing."

"That's okay, tell me if he inquiries about her again."

"I will."

Emma and Henrietta got their coats and headed down the elevator. Once they got to the lobby, the duo waved to the guard. They pulled on their coats and hats; Emma wrapped the scarf around Henrietta and put hers on.

They quickly headed outside and the driver looked impatient. "You know how cold it is and my horse can't be out here forever."

"We're sorry. Can we go?" Emma said shortly.

The driver opened the door and they got in quickly with his help.

"He sure is in a bad mood," Henrietta said once they got moving.

"I can't blame him; it's the weather and he's concerned about his horse. I was the one in the wrong here."

Henrietta stared at Emma for a long moment and said, "I never heard an adult admit to any blame."

"I'll always tell you when I'm the one at fault."

"I'll do the same," Henrietta promised.

"Great. Henrietta, we never asked you how you felt about moving in with us, about how Jeremy and I want to be your guardians."

"It's the best thing that's ever happened to me. My parents never really wanted me. They wanted Aiden. Even then, they had both of us working as early as they could."

"We won't do that to you."

"I know that," Henrietta said and wiped her eyes. She moved her hand to Emma's and held it tightly.

They pulled to a stop at the boarding house. Emma said, "Go on in and I'll pay the driver."

"You should give him a good tip."

"I will," she promised. "Be careful getting down."

Henrietta opened the door and, surprisingly, the driver was there to help them down. "Thank you," said Henrietta over the wind. Emma took his hand and was glad for the support out to the carriage.

Once down, she said. "I apologize for leaving you out in the weather."

"Thanks."

She took out her purse and handed him his fee and added a hefty tip.

He looked at the large tip Emma had given him. "Thank you for this."

"Get yourself and that horse somewhere warm."

"I will," he said and pulled himself up into the driver's seat.

She watched him go and then slowly made her way to the stoop. "Need a hand?" a voice came from behind her. She started to turn quickly and her foot slipped.

"Watch out!" Jeremy grabbed her by the collar to stabilize her. "Got it?"

"I think so."

"Let's go up together." They went slowly and finally made it to the door and inside. "Finally," she said, pulling off her scarf and hat.

"Was something up with the driver?" asked Jeremy. He'd been dropped off close to them and saw they were in a conversation.

"Yes, I left him outside too long when I was picking up Henrietta."

"You have to watch that in this weather," he cautioned.

"I know, I got distracted."

"By what?" he asked curiously.

"Clair wanted to talk about the party at Geoff's home."

"Were she and Thomas invited?"

"No. It looks like it's just the people we already know about."

Dora called to them from the dining room. "Clean up the snow and come into dinner."

Emma rolled her eyes and handed him her outer gear and picked up a broom that was nearby. She swept the snow into a pan and saw the wind still whipping up outside. "I need to move this to the kitchen."

Jeremy followed her to the dining room and took his chair while she disposed of the snow in the kitchen sink. The dinner smells diverted her attention and she said to Amy, "It smells amazing."

"Here, take this in and we can get dinner started," Amy offered.

Emma took the tray of meat from her and headed into the dining room. She was closely followed by Amy with pitchers of tea and water and Ethyl with the soup.

Everyone sat at the table and, even though it wasn't Monday, Savannah and Ethan were there. She'd opted out of the Christmas show so she could concentrate on the wedding plans.

Emma noticed that there was a large bowl of biscuits sitting next to Henrietta's plate. Dora had made sure Henrietta knew they'd keep their promises to her.

Emma sat and looked over at Savannah. "Savannah, your dresses are completed if you want to do a final fitting after dinner."

"That would be wonderful."

"We also need to go over the guest list and food," Dora reminded her sister.

Henrietta spoke up. "I need some help with my homework."

Emma looked torn. "I can handle it," Jeremy said and winked at her. Henrietta looked relieved.

Emma leaned closer to him. "Thanks."

"We have to share responsibilities now."

CHAPTER 13

Nathan sat at his desk opening correspondence.

Geoff stepped out of his office and casually asked, "Is Henrietta back at the office?"

Nathan didn't look up but continued to record the envelopes he'd opened. "Yes, Lily mentioned that she'd returned to work today."

Then she must have returned to school, Geoff thought. *Good.* As he walked back to his office, Nathan spoke again.

"I saw Emma going up there earlier and Lily said that Emma and Jeremy are her guardians now."

It was all he could not to rub his hands together in glee. *Things are coming together.* As Geoff left his office, Nathan looked at the door he'd gone through and narrowed his eyes.

CHAPTER 14

That evening at Geoff and Gregory's apartment

Geoff entered the apartment and walked quickly toward the music. He found Gregory, as expected, at the piano.

Gregory spotted him and, when he saw the expression on his friend's face, he stopped playing. He slowly closed the piano key cover and looked at him expectantly. "Well?"

Geoff didn't say anything. Instead, he smiled and walked over to the drinks that were set out on a small cocktail table.

Gregory knew that Geoff liked to drag things out, so he waited patiently. They'd played this scene more than once in their relationship.

"She hasn't questioned the party." Geoff laughed and toasted Gregory.

"She hasn't? Then you think she doesn't expect anything?"

"No, my plans are on track."

Gregory started to finger-tap out one of his songs on the top of the piano. "Isn't this too risky and too close to home?"

"It has to be here and with this group. Don't you see? It's the ultimate challenge. The others were just in preparation for this." He took a drink and looked over at Gregory. "And doing this here will give you something you want."

Gregory nodded and his finger stopped moving. "What if we do all of this and I still don't get her?"

"You will," Geoff said confidently.

Will I? he thought.

CHAPTER 15

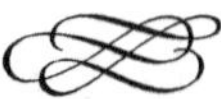

After dinner that night, Dora, Tim, and Emma sat around the kitchen table reviewing their business accounts. Jeremy was with Henrietta in the dining room; they were making good progress through her backlog of homework. Jake sat across the table reviewing his photography books; he liked to keep Ethyl company while she finished her evening duties.

Tim started with employees at local stores, offices, maids, and housemen. "We're good with employment, but we're short-staffed for some parties coming up."

"Which ones?" Dora asked.

" Geoff and Gregory's party, for one. They've requested staff for a week and a half before the party."

"How many?"

Tim looked through his notes. "Says here they're requesting kitchen help and a server. I believe he also wants them to put out the decorations. There's something odd about the request."

"What's that?" Emma asked, her eyes narrowing.

"They only want someone during the evenings. No one during the day."

"I wonder why?" asked Dora. "They could get more cleaning done in the day. Evenings will be limited."

"And that will be hard to fill," Emma commented.

"I could do it," Ethyl volunteered from behind them.

Tim turned toward her with a frown on his face and asked, "You wouldn't mind working two jobs? Leaving here and then working there every night?"

"Well, it would only be for a few weeks. And I could use some extra money for Christmas." She'd been looking at a special camera for Jake's gift. She had it on hold but didn't have the money to pick it up yet.

Tim tapped his page with his pen. "That still leaves us one person down to help. It would be too much for Ethyl by herself."

Jake cleared his throat. Dora asked, "Jake, you wanted to say something?"

"I can help her," he said, his tone even with no inflection.

"You can?" Tim asked. Jake had never worked for their business; he worked for the local police department, photographing crime scenes.

"I can."

Ethyl walked over to stand behind Jake. "I can direct him."

Tim and Dora's eyes met, and she gave a small nod. Tim caught it and said, "I think that can work. Can you both start tomorrow night?"

Ethyl put her hand on Jake's shoulder. "We can. Are the decorations already there?"

"I'll contact Geoff and see if he can have them moved. Do you have a uniform for the party?"

"I don't," she said as she moved her hands to nervously twist her apron strings.

"That's okay," Dora told her. "We have a black dress and white apron that will do."

"Is this okay when I'm working there before the party?" Ethyl asked, indicating her dress.

"That should be fine," Emma said, "since it's in the evening and will probably be just Geoff and Gregory."

"And we'll help you with transportation to and from the building," Dora added.

"Thank you!" Ethyl said, relieved.

"No, the thanks are to you and Jake. We won't have any shortages of help this season."

The group finished their discussion and they disbanded. Savannah, Emma, and Dora completed a final fitting. There were only a few details needed to finish both garments.

Emma moved to the sitting groom to continue working on the hem of Savannah's party dress. It just required a little shortening. Jake and Ethyl were pulling on their coats and walked into the foyer. Emma put down her sewing and joined them. "Ethyl, could I ask you a favor?"

"Of course," said Ethyl.

"Don't mention where your day job is located."

Ethyl tilted her head. "It shouldn't matter; most families that hire help don't talk to us much. As long as we get the work done."

"Except us," she teased.

Ethyl's face turned red. "Yes, you're the exception."

Emma laughed. "Well, if they do ask, make sure to keep it vague."

"I will," she promised and turned toward the door.

"One more thing," Emma added.

"Yes?" she asked as she turned back to her.

"If you hear or see anything suspicious, you'll let me know."

Ethyl lowered her voice. "Is something bad going on there?" She knew Emma and the rest often helped the police and Pinkerton Agency solve crimes.

"I don't think so; it's just odd," Emma admitted.

"Ethyl," called Jake. He was dressed and ready to go.

"On my way." She turned to Emma one last time. "I'll update you." She buttoned her coat and walked to Jake.

"Hat and scarf," he reminded her.

She nodded and pulled them on. "Better?" she asked.

"Yes, just right." They walked out together.

"Jake, be careful coming back," Emma warned.

"I will." He knew that, if he was too delayed, Tim would go meet him.

Emma went back to the sitting room to continue her work on Savannah's party dress hem. She absently listened to the conversation between Henrietta and Jeremy. Her homework was becoming entertaining.

"Hen, I don't think you're supposed to take sides in your report," Jeremy said.

"I don't see why not."

"What're you two discussing?" Emma asked them.

"Frankenstein's Monster. She's taking his side and thinks his rights are being violated."

Emma smothered a laugh and said, "Hen, just write the report and probably leave your opinions out."

"But don't you agree the monster should have been treated better?"

"I do," Emma agreed. "And if another person is created in real life out of different body parts, I'll be right there to support him and you."

"See," Hen said to Jeremy triumphantly. "She agrees with me."

Jeremy shook his head at both of them. "Get to work. This is a ridiculous conversation."

Emma smiled. Jeremy was enjoying the interaction each evening. And she admitted to herself, it was nice for her also.

CHAPTER 16

The next evening, Ethyl and Jake would be at Geoff and Gregory's apartment for the first time. Emma watched them in the hallway. Tim had the wagon waiting. He'd take them over and then pick them up in a few hours.

Emma was on edge, watching the clock until bedtime. She couldn't stay up any longer and went to bed. The next morning, she woke quickly and glanced at the clock. It was early and bread day, so she knew Amy and Ethyl would be hard at work downstairs. She dressed quickly without disturbing Jeremy and headed downstairs.

The house was quiet and she carried her boots in one hand. She sat in the dining room and pulled on her boots before entering the kitchen. She pushed the door open slowly, not wanting to startle Amy or Ethyl. As she expected, they were both there working on different types of bread and pastry.

Amy noticed her and said, "Emma, you're up early."

"Yeah, I hoped to talk to Ethyl about her new job."

Amy motioned with her hand. "As long as the baking keeps going." She wouldn't mention anything she heard; she'd been with them a long time and understood the nature of the investigations they participated in.

"Tell me about last night," said Emma.

Ethyl continued to manipulate the dough as she started to tell her about the night before. "Jake and I arrived on time and Mr. Beeker and Mr. Walker were already there."

"Who gave you instructions on your task?"

"Mr. Beeker did. Mr. Walker was playing the piano while we were there."

"What were your duties last night?"

"We were told to come in and clean, and we're to do that each night. Mr. Beeker will have the decorations brought up tomorrow. We're to put them out and decorate the tree. On the day of the party, we'll bring cookies and pastries. I'll make chicken and vegetables for the guests."

"Flowers," Jake said from the doorway. He moved to his place at the kitchen table.

Ethyl smiled at him and said, "Yes, that's true, we'll need flowers. We'll pick them up when we get the pastries and cookies." She finished working the dough and put it in a bowl and pulled a towel over it. She moved on to cutting the bacon.

"One more thing," Emma said, "do you think you could map out the apartment for me?"

"What for?"

"I don't know, and let me know if there are any changes you see between now and the party."

"Large changes?"

"It could be large or small."

Ethyl nodded. "Jake is good with details. He can help."

"I am," he acknowledged.

Emma looked at Jake and back at Ethyl. "Thanks."

"Is this a case?" Jake asked.

"I honestly don't know," Emma admitted, "just some things about the party that are making me uncomfortable."

"We'll map out the area on my break," Ethyl assured her.

"I'll check with you after breakfast."

Emma went back upstairs to read for a while before Jeremy woke up. She opened the door and was surprised to see Jeremy sitting up in bed reading. He closed the book and asked, "Where did you go so early?"

"Just down to ask Ethyl about her job last night."

"What about it?" he asked with a frown.

"I asked her to tell me if they saw anything out of the ordinary."

"And did they?"

"No."

"But you're still wondering if this is something other than what it appears to be?"

"For now," she allowed.

He shook his head and went back to his book. She pulled off her boots and joined him on the bed, grabbing her book from the side table.

After breakfast, Ethyl gave Emma the layout. It was detailed and showed all of the main furniture for the room.

Perfect, she thought. *It's like a chess game and now I know what the board looks like.* She kept studying the paper during breakfast.

"What is that?" Tim asked.

"Nothing," Emma said. She took the paper and placed it in her pocket. Jeremy watched the move and, when breakfast was finished, he said, "I need to go upstairs for a minute. Come with me."

"I have everything I need," she said.

"I don't and I think you might need something also."

She squinted at his tone and accompanied him upstairs.

He left her at her door and motioned to her to go in.

She went in and thought, *Okay, what's going on?*

The bookshelf hiding the door opened quickly and he came

in. He didn't say anything. Instead, he sat on the bed, sighed, and fell backward.

"Is there something you wanted to discuss?" she asked and leaned against the door.

Instead of answering, he asked, "What's on that paper?"

She reached into her pocket and pulled the map out. She walked over to the bed and handed it to him.

He unfolded it. "What is this?"

"A map of Geoff and Gregory's apartment."

He sat up. "Are you investigating them?"

"No," she said slowly. "Not really, I'm just watching."

"What do you have?"

"I don't know. An uncomfortable feeling; a lot of things that aren't adding up. There's Gregory and Savannah's last meeting and then the stranger inquiring about Hen at school."

He sighed again and laid back down. "Do you have time to go to Pop's house with me this morning? I think it's time you were briefed on something."

Her eyebrows raised, and she said, "I can make the time."

"Good. Let's go." He went through the bookcase and didn't look back.

She stared as he disappeared into his room, then shrugged and went to her door. He was waiting there for her. They started down the stairs and he held out his hand to her. She took it without hesitation. They were always a team, even if they disagreed about something.

"I'll get our coats," he said.

"I'll get our lunches."

She went to the kitchen and saw Dora waiting there. "Did you forget something?" she asked.

"Yeah, lunches," said Emma, grabbing them.

"I mean something else."

"She means me," Henrietta piped up from behind Dora.

Emma turned slowly to the small girl. "I'm so sorry, Henrietta, I got distracted. Are you finished with breakfast?"

"Yes." Hen's mouth was turned down and she was kicking her foot and hitting a cupboard door.

Emma went over to her and tilted her head up. "I'm sorry, baby, this is still new to me. To us. You'll occasionally have to remind me when I get distracted. Can you do that?"

She pursed her lips. "I can. But can you try harder?"

"I can. Come on." Emma reached over and grabbed her lunch and carried the three pails out.

Jeremy had pulled out three coats; he'd remembered. She rolled her eyes at him and helped Henrietta with her coat.

"You could have reminded me, you muttonhead," she whispered at him as he helped her with her coat.

"Muttonhead? You wound me, madam," he said, chuckling.

Once suitably dressed, they exited the house to the waiting carriage. He gave the addresses to the driver and climbed in beside Henrietta and Emma.

They took Henrietta to school first and Emma walked her in. She stopped the girl and asked, "Are we good?"

"Yes."

She leaned in for a kiss and Henrietta asked, "See you at Clair's?"

"Of course."

"And you don't mind spending time at the bakery with me this evening?"

"I can't wait."

"You like the pastries," she teased her.

"I do."

The girl looked more cheerful and Emma said, "I have to go. Have a great day." She watched her enter the class. Then she headed back out to the waiting carriage.

"Everything okay?" Jeremy asked.

"Except for me forgetting her this morning."

"Hey, ease up a little. We're new at this," he reminded her.

"You remembered! I didn't; it shouldn't have happened."

"Hmm, maybe you should write it down in your notebook."

"Maybe I will."

They were silent for the rest of the trip to Cole's house. Once there, he told the carriage he could go.

"What about work?" she asked.

"We can ride in with Pops."

They started up the steps. Emma couldn't wait for the meeting with Cole and pulled on Jeremy's arm to stop him. "Jeremy, what's this about?"

"Wait until we get in. Just a few more moments. Trust me?"

She nodded. "Always."

They entered the house without knocking. They could hear laughter coming from the dining room. "Pops!" called Jeremy.

Cole came to the doorway and waved to them. "Good to see you. Join us here. Coffee?"

They entered the dining room and saw that Ellis and Abbey were there also. Cole, Abbey, and Ellis shared a house. They'd been friends for many years.

Jeremy went to Abbey and kissed her cheek. "Morning, Mom."

"Good morning, Jeremy."

"Little girl," Ellis said as he stood to kiss her on the cheek. "What brings you here this morning?"

"Not me," Emma said. "Jeremy said we needed to see Cole."

Cole put down his coffee. "Jeremy, what's this about?" he asked.

"Can we go somewhere to talk?"

"Of course. Excuse us a moment," he said to Ellis and Abbey.

"Come see us after you've finished," Abbey told the duo.

"We will," promised Emma.

Cole led the way to the study. They entered and Cole pulled

the doors closed behind them. Emma raised her brows but stayed silent.

"Pop, she needs to be read in on the case," Jeremy began.

Cole looked at him, "Son. we promised the client we wouldn't share this information with anyone."

"We have to or the whole thing will be exposed too early."

"Would someone just tell me already!" Emma said, clearly exasperated.

Cole walked over to a large brown chair across from the couch where Emma and Jeremy sat down. "Clair contacted us."

"Clair! What has she to do with this?"

"She contacted us six months ago."

"Six months! Why?"

"She'd been watching the finances carefully since the incident with Zeke's son, Sam Peterson, made her doubt her skills at running the foundation." Emma started to protest but Cole raised his hand. "I agree she wasn't in the wrong, but she had a theory about the missing money that I thought was worth investigating."

Emma thought about who handled the finances for the foundation and suddenly things started coming together. "Is it Geoff? It is, isn't it?" she asked.

Jeremy grinned. He and Cole had been working on this case for six months and Emma had made the connection in no time. "Yes. Zeke's son would have needed someone with bank contacts to siphon money off like he was. We were suspicious enough to look into it."

"But we audited Geoff's firm in New York and didn't find anything that concerned us," Emma said.

"That's why we needed someone to be there undercover to see if there was anything to find."

She thought about who was in the office. It could only be the secretary. "Nathan?"

"Yes. We needed someone who had both a sketchy background and training in accounting. Nathan fit that exactly," explained Jeremy.

"Is he Pinkerton?

Cole laughed. "He is now."

"Hmm," said Emma.

"Jeremy, tell me why you thought Emma should be read in now."

"It's the party that Geoff and Gregory are throwing. Emma's concerned there's something else happening."

"What is it that's bothering you about it?" Cole asked.

"There isn't a lot," she muttered.

"Tell me," he prompted. Her intuition had led them to many cases being resolved.

"This party has never been here in Chicago."

"Is it always in the same place?"

"No, but never here."

"You were never invited to those?"

"Never. And the list of invitees is odd."

"Who's on this list?"

"Me, Jeremy, Dora, Tim, Savannah, Ethan, and Savannah's parents."

"Is that an odd group?" Cole asked.

"Not really," said Jeremy. "Dora, Tim, and Emma know Geoff. And Gregory knows Savannah and her parents from the theatre."

"Hmm. Is that all?"

"Savannah mentioned that she and Gregory weren't on the best terms. The last time she'd seen him, he asked her out and she turned him down. He didn't take it well."

"Yet Savannah, Ethan, and her parents are going?" Cole asked.

"Yes."

"What else?" he asked, sitting forward.

She started to frown. "What is it?" asked Jeremy.

"There's the Hen element."

"Hen?" Cole asked.

"Henrietta, the girl we're now guardians of," said Jeremy.

"Yes, yes. How is she involved in this?" asked Cole.

"A few days ago, a man was at the school and had asked about her address. Lily mentioned that Nathan had asked about the name of her school before that," said Emma.

"She told him?" Jeremy asked her.

"It wasn't a secret."

"And you think that was Geoff?" Cole asked.

"Well, the description the school gave us could have been anyone. But yes, I do. Things are just adding up."

"What could be the reason for all of this?"

Emma stood and walked to the desk and turned back to them. "Hen feels like a pawn, to be used and discarded."

"We'd never do that," Jeremy assured her.

"I know we wouldn't, but Geoff might."

"What else?" asked Cole.

"I think she may be used as a distraction for me and Jeremy."

Cole asked, "What's happened since he inquired about her?"

Jeremy answered. "She was pulled out of school by her parents, and they placed her in a factory to work. Then we went to their house."

Something occurred to Emma. "Jeremy, do you remember what Hen's father said?"

"I do. *'He said "I told you".'*"

"We were too distracted when we were there to followup."

"It did stop you from going to Geoff's office," Jeremy reminded her.

"That's true."

"Pops, can Nathan check for a payment from Geoff to Hen's parents?"

"I'll check with him," confirmed Cole.

"Do we send our regrets and get everyone else to also?" asked Jeremy.

"We're too close to the party and the close of the case. And he may get suspicious of Nathan," Cole replied.

"Because Nathan's the one who knows Geoff asked about Hen."

"Yes."

"I'd like to see this through," Emma said.

"Then you both go to the party and keep your eyes open and we finish the investigation," Cole said.

"When do you expect your investigation to end?" she asked.

Jeremy said, "The January report detailing the year will be put out at the end of December."

"What'll that prove?" she asked.

"Nathan has the actual numbers that should be released. When the report goes out, we'll have proof that the numbers don't match. We'll use that to arrest him."

"If there are two sets of books, why not confront him now?"

"We need the proof that that report will provide," said Cole.

" Geoff doesn't know about Nathan, so I don't think the foundation is involved in whatever is supposed to happen at the party," said Emma.

"No," said Cole. "This party seems direct and more personal."

"But aimed at who?" Jeremy asked.

"Someone in our group," said Emma.

Cole said, "Let me follow up with Nathan and see what he thinks this is about. He might have some theories. You'll let me know if anything else changes?"

She nodded. "Please let me know what Nathan says."

Cole pulled open the doors and walked back toward the dining room.

Emma and Jeremy lagged behind. He took her hand and pulled her to a stop. "What's your main worry?"

"Right now? I don't know. Geoff's distractions are working and I can't put my finger on what is going on."

"It may be that we allow things to happen when we get there. It will be eventful."

"Yes, it looks like a party to remember."

He nodded and offered her his elbow and escorted her into the dining room.

Abbey and Papa sat at the table; Cole had joined them for coffee.

Jeremy helped Emma with her seat and took one for himself.

"We have a wedding coming up," Abbey said excitedly.

"Yes," Emma agreed, grateful for the happier topic. "Savannah and Ethan are looking forward to their day."

"Christmas Eve?" Papa asked.

"Yes, that's what they wanted. We thought to have it by candlelight and then the reception after."

"It does sound wonderful," Abbey said. "Have you and Dora completed her dress?" Abbey had seen the initial sketches that included Emma's custom lace designs.

"I've been distracted, but I'll be spending most nights up until the wedding on it."

"Will you get it finished?"

"We will."

Papa asked, "When will we decorate the house? And get to meet the new member of our family?"

The family would pull together and decorate the boarding house for Christmas. "Dora mentioned trees this morning and getting the boxes from the attic," Emma replied. "She should be sending over a note soon. And we can't wait for you to meet Henrietta."

"We can't wait to meet her." Abbey bit her lip and said, "We're getting close to Christmas. Ellis, Cole, we should also be getting our tree set up."

"We'll go tomorrow," Ellis promised.

Cole said, "I'll have the boxes brought down from the attic. The holidays are coming up faster than I realized."

"Yes, it is," said Emma, thinking of not just Christmas, but also the wedding and *the* party.

Cole noticed the time and went to look out the windows by the front door. He turned back to them. "The carriage is here. Emma, we can drop you off at Pennington's on the way."

Emma and Jeremy joined him in the foyer and pulled on their coats, hats, and scarves. The wind had picked up again. Cole got to the carriage first and shouted to the driver over the wind, "I'll hold the door!" He held the door and Jeremy helped lift Emma into the vehicle.

They climbed in behind her and Jeremy pulled the door closed. Cole sat across from them and used his umbrella to tap the ceiling to indicate he could move on.

Emma huddled next to Jeremy and he pulled her in close. They were all thinking of their discussion in the study. *Who is Geoff really? Is Gregory part of this?*

They dropped Emma off at her office; Jeremy kissed her quickly and climbed back into the carriage to head to the Pinkerton offices. She pushed her way up the stoop and leaned on the door to open it. It swung open with the lightest pressure and she went face-first into a man's coat.

"I'm sorry," she started and turned to push the door closed. Once the weather was outside and not inside, she turned back and reached up to unwind her scarf.

She paused with her hand raised and saw John Harden in the office! Emma started to reach for her knife and remembered she didn't carry it with her to work. "What the hell are you doing here?" she demanded.

Harden looked at her with a hurt expression. "Emma, you know I was released. Good behavior and all." He smiled wolfishly.

"And all," she muttered, removing the last of the scarf from her face. "Is there a reason you're here?"

"Emma," Pennington called out, "no questions. Mr. Harden is a client."

A client? Emma frowned and started to open her mouth.

John laughed, delighted. "You've managed to do something I never have been able to, silence Emma Evans."

Emma stared, staying quiet as he took hold of the door handle. "I'm looking forward to working with you," he said to Pennington, but kept his eyes on hers.

"Us also. Please let me know if you'd like to meet again before the holiday," Pennington said.

"I will," he promised. He put on his hat and tilted it toward her as he moved outside. "Emma," he murmured.

"John," she murmured back, disgusted, and watched him leave. Once the door closed, she whirled around to Mr. Pennington. "What was that? We're working for HIM?"

"In my office, please," he said.

"But… but," she stuttered.

"Office. Now," he said firmly.

She wanted to argue but instead started toward his office.

Ethan piped up from his desk. "You can hang up your coat first."

She startled; she hadn't removed her coat or her hat. Once they had been placed in the closet, she took out her notebook and headed to Pennington's office. She sent Ethan a questioning look; he shrugged but didn't offer any further information.

The office door stood open and she took a deep breath and entered. Mr. Pennington waved at his table. She sat and waited. He picked up a file, closed the door, and sat across from her.

He leaned back and said, "We've added Mr. Harden as a client. Will that be an issue for you?"

"I guess that depends on what capacity we are to be working for him." Emma knew her boss was well aware of John's prior residence—prison—as well as who and what had helped put him there.

"That's fair," he allowed. "I can alleviate your concerns with that topic. He has just put us on retainer for any future projects."

"No current issues?"

"No. He's purchasing several properties here and will want us to steer him through the process."

"That sounds fine," she said, drumming her fingers on her lips.

"Emma, we don't investigate clients unless they ask us to," he said, guessing at her thoughts.

"No, it's not that. I do like the idea that he's purchasing the properties through the proper channels and not illegal ones. Did he say what the properties will be used as?"

"No, but there's no reason why I can't share the information with you. It will be a matter of public record."

She started to stand and he stopped her. "One more thing. I have something for Savannah and Ethan's wedding."

"What is it?"

"A three-week trip to New York."

"They'll love that."

"I want to show him that I value his work."

"Have you told him?"

"Not yet. I thought we could go out to lunch."

Emma knew that Savannah came to see Ethan at lunch during rehearsals.

"That will be nice. "

"Could you tell Ethan we want to eat lunch together with them?"

"I will." She stood, knowing they'd finished their meeting.

With the door closed behind her, she moved to Ethan's desk and leaned on it. His face was buried in a file on his desk. She waited until he looked over at her.

"What are you staring at? Shouldn't you be getting to work?"

"I should," she allowed, not straightening.

"Was there something else?" he asked.

"Is Savannah coming for lunch today?"

He frowned a bit at the change of topic. "Yes, I expect her at the normal time."

"Good, Mr. Pennington and I'd like to have lunch with you both."

Ethan was not one to question Mr. Pennington and he nodded. "I'll put it on the calendar."

She hid a smile with her hand and headed to her office. He called behind her, "Your files are on your desk. Turn them in before we leave. I need to get them to the court this afternoon."

"I'll get them ready," she said and walked into her office. It was the smallest but it was somewhere she could work in private. She hoped the morning would be quiet; sometimes the outer office could have many clients waiting.

Unfortunately, this morning was no different. She could hear people arguing as they entered the office. She could feel the walls shake when the outer door slammed. There was no need to open her door to hear the argument occurring in the outer office.

She knew who these men were; a client had passed away and his sons were fighting over the will. Last time they'd visited, they'd gotten into fisticuffs and Ethan had to stand between the brothers to stop the fight.

"He thinks he's better than me!"

Great, they're here, she thought. *And I'm staying right where I am.*

"Emma!" Ethan yelled for her. "Emma, help!"

Well, I thought I was. She jumped up and ran into the room. Once there, she found Ethan between the two brothers and they were reaching over him to hit each other. Mr. Pennington came out of his office at the same time. He motioned for her to handle one of the brothers. She grabbed one by the collar and turned his arm up his back. Mr. Pennington took the other brother and shook him. "Stop it! If you continue like this, I won't represent either of you."

They both stopped struggling; Mr. Pennington and Emma released them.

"Into my office, both of you. NOW!" He treated the men like the recalcitrant children they were. They looked down at the floor and followed him in.

Once his door was closed, Emma turned to Ethan. "What's the problem with those two?"

"The younger brother thinks that his brother isn't smart enough to run the estate. The fights start when the younger one disagrees with how the money's being spent. Mr. Pennington evaluates the decision and gives them his opinion."

"Is the younger one smarter?"

"He's more clever, which makes the other brother more desperate."

She shook her head and went back to her office. The lunch hour was approaching and she went into the outer office to find out if they were leaving at noon. The door to Mr. Pennington's office opened at the same time and the brothers exited. They were much quieter than when they arrived. They seemed to have reached an agreement, though the older brother looked unhappy. Mr. Pennington escorted them to the door.

Once it was closed, he wiped his forehead. "Lord, if it wasn't for their parents, I wouldn't keep them as clients." He glanced out the windows by the door. "Grab your coats. I see Savannah coming up."

Savannah came in and unwrapped her scarf. When she started to work on the buttons of her coat, Ethan stopped her. "Leave it on, we're going to lunch with Mr. Pennington and Emma."

"Really? That would be nice," she said with a large smile. She walked over and kissed Ethan on his cheek. He turned red but he didn't pull away.

Pennington pulled on his coat, as did Emma and Ethan. He'd arranged for a carriage to take them to a nice restaurant. "If we're ready, the carriage is here." Everyone headed to the door, wrapping their scarves tightly around their faces. The wind had continued and the snow had started again.

They got to their destination and sat. It was nicer than Ethan expected and his eyes widened when they arrived. Mr. Pennington noticed and assured him, "Don't worry, my boy, I'm paying the check."

Ethan was relieved. "Thank you, sir."

They ordered and, as they were waiting, Mr. Pennington said, "I want to congratulate you and Savannah on your wedding."

"Thank you, sir," he said.

"Thank you, Mr. Pennington," said Savannah.

"I heard you won't be taking a trip after the wedding."

"We're saving for a trip," she replied. Ethan nodded.

"Well, maybe I can help with that," Pennington said, pulling out a large envelope. "These are train tickets to New York. Also included is the hotel where you'll stay and money for food and other essentials."

Savannah started to cry and Ethan said, "Sir, thank you so much for doing this."

"You're very valuable to me and my office. I want you to be happy and I know Savannah makes you happy."

"She does," Ethan said, taking her hand in his.

"Take this. I arranged it for you to leave on December 26."

"Sir, what about the office?" Ethan asked, opening the envelope.

"We'll be closed."

"Closed?" Ethan and Emma asked together. They'd never closed for three weeks before this.

"Yes, I'm going to take a vacation also." Pennington didn't comment where he was going; he could be a private man on personal matters.

Their meal was delivered and the conversation continued around the table. Emma gave them advice on what they should see on their trip. Savannah and Ethan had lots of questions and the lunch went quickly. After the meal was over, they headed back to the office. Once there, Pennington and Emma went to their respective offices to give Ethan and Savannah time to talk.

Now left alone, Savannah fell into Ethan's arms. "A week in New York," Ethan said wonderingly.

"And two weeks to ourselves in a private car on the train," Savannah said suggestively.

"It was thoughtful of Mr. Pennington to do that for us." They kissed. Ethan pushed her back and said, "Now that I know the office will be closed, I'll need to put in some extra time getting the clients' folders organized and closed for the year."

"We do have some parties before the wedding," she reminded him.

"I know. I'll make the time," he promised.

Pennington walked out. "Ethan," he started. He stopped when he saw Savannah was still there. "I'm sorry, I didn't want to interrupt."

"No, sir," Savannah assured him, "I have to get to the theatre. I'm turning over some of my stage managing duties to my replacement and now I need to get the time off for a trip. Thank you again."

"My pleasure."

"I'll be going, I know you're busy," she said to Ethan. He buttoned her coat up and she pulled down her hat and wrapped her scarf around her neck. "Tonight?"

"I'll meet you at the boarding house," he agreed.

"Remember, we're decorating tonight. Tim picked up the trees this morning."

"I'll be there."

Mr. Pennington pulled on his coat. "Are you ready?" They had court that afternoon.

"Emma!" called Ethan.

Emma came through her door with a stack of files. "I have them ready."

Ethan took them and placed them in his bag.

"We will be in court all afternoon," Mr. Pennington told Emma.

"Yes, sir. I will work on my files, then head to the bakery."

He nodded and the small group headed out to the carriage. They would go to court and then have the carriage take Savannah to the theatre.

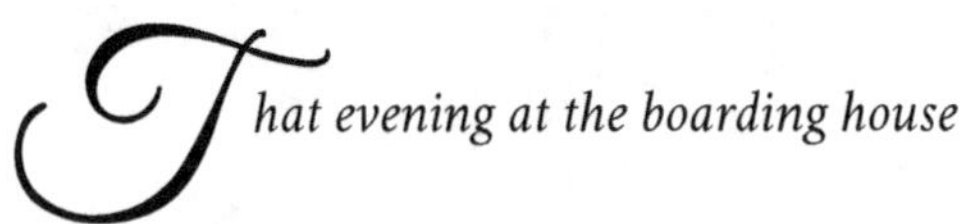

hat evening at the boarding house

Dora was directing Tim and Jake. "The larger tree goes into the foyer."

"And the small one into the sitting room," teased Tim.

"Yes," she said and watched them closely. They placed the tree on the stand and Dora stood back to look at it. "To the right." Once they got it the way she wanted it, they moved to the sitting room. Tim and Jake gripped the tree and, when they started to move it, they heard a knock at the door. Dora glanced toward it; she was torn; she wanted to get the tree into the right spot.

"Jake, set the tree down," Tim said. Jake did as he was told.

The knock sounded at the door again. "Want me to get it?" Jake asked. Dora was still studying the tree without comment.

Tim smiled slightly and said, "Please."

Jake ran to the door and opened it. A group of people

crowded into the foyer. Tim pulled Dora away from the tree and they walked to the foyer to welcome their guests.

"Papa," she said and went to him first to kiss him on the cheek. "Abbey, you look lovely," she remarked to her stepmother.

Tim greeted Cole. "Welcome."

"We're glad to be inside," he said as Tim took their coats and stowed them in the hall closet.

Abbey went to the tall tree in the foyer. "It's wonderful Dora. We need to get ours and decorate it." She shot a disapproving look at Ellis and Cole.

Ellis sighed. "We'll get the boxes down tomorrow morning, dear."

"That would be nice," she said.

"Let's move into the sitting room," Dora suggested.

"Will dinner be soon?" asked Jake. He liked to stay on schedule.

Dora put her hand on his arm. "Soon. We're waiting for Jeremy to pick up Emma and Henrietta from the bakery."

"Ethyl and I have to leave after dinner; we won't be able to stay and decorate," he reminded her.

"We'll miss you. Would you like me to save you some cookies?" Dora asked.

"Yes, please."

Abbey perked up. "We heard that Henrietta is now Jeremy's and Emma's ward. What's she like?"

Dora smiled. "She is a nice girl, and so good with Lottie."

"Smart, too," Tim added. "She's excelling at school."

Cole explained to Abbey and Ellis, "Jeremy met Henrietta during his investigation of the glass factory. Her brother, Aiden, had died in an accident there."

"Those poor children," Abbey exclaimed. "I hate that someone couldn't have stopped that."

"Jeremy continues to check in on them from time to time

and hold them to their breaks, schedules, and other safety concerns."

Just then, the door banged open and they could hear more people entering the foyer.

"They're here! Now we can eat," Jake said.

"Why don't you go tell Amy and Ethyl we'll be wanting to eat soon," Dora suggested.

He nodded and headed that way.

Emma, Jeremy, and Henrietta came into the sitting room. "We have cookies," said Emma, holding up the boxes.

"And other treats," Henrietta said.

"Hen! Hen!" called Lottie. Henrietta handed her boxes to Jeremy, went over, and picked the girl up.

"Take those in to Amy; we'll put them on trays for when we start decorating," directed Dora.

Jake walked back into the room. "Let's go! Dinner has started to be moved to the table."

Dora grinned and turned to the group. "Well, it appears we are ready."

As the group started to move toward the dining room, Jeremy said, "Mom, Pops, Ellis, this is Henrietta. She'll live with us from now on."

Abbey looked at the young girl closely and said, "I understand you're very smart."

"I am," she said proudly.

"She is," Emma said. "She's already completed the two weeks' worth of work she missed to catch up on her studies."

"I'm learning to bake also," Henrietta said.

"Did you make some of the cookies we're having tonight?" Abbey asked.

"I helped Emma make them."

"She did. I couldn't have gotten as much done if she hadn't been there," Emma said.

"It's very nice to meet you," Cole said.

"Thank you," Henrietta replied.

Abbey said, "I understand that you need some new clothes."

Hen bit her lip; she didn't want to ask for anything.

Emma saw her reaction and said, "She does. We've just been so busy."

"Is school out soon?"

"The last day is tomorrow," confirmed Jeremy. He and Emma were monitoring Hen's schedule closely.

"Then would you like to go with me to my seamstress appointment the day after? We can get you some school dresses and a nice dress for the wedding."

"Really?" Henrietta looked at Emma and Jeremy. They nodded.

Emma's eyes filled with tears and she turned to hide them. Henrietta hadn't had new clothes before, and the few things she considered hers had been taken by her parents. Jeremy put a hand on her shoulder. "Are you okay?" he asked in a low voice.

"I am," she said and gave him a quick kiss. "I think they're waiting on us for dinner."

Dora called from the dining room, "Dinner is on the table. "

As they walked to the table, Savannah rushed into the house. She quickly put her coat up and walked into the room with the others. "Sorry I'm a little late. There was a lot of snow tonight. Is Ethan here yet?" she asked and looked around for him.

"Not yet," Emma replied. "Do you want us to wait for him?"

"No, he may have to work late, but he should be here soon. I'll get with Amy to put a plate together for him," she said as she walked into the kitchen.

The family took their seats and, once Savannah returned, they said prayers, then platters were passed around.

Abbey turned to Savannah. "May I see your wedding dress tonight?"

Savannah looked at Emma and Dora for their guidance. "Of

course," said Dora. "If you want to try it on after we decorate, we can confirm everything is completed."

Once dinner was started, Amy came to Dora and reminded them they needed to leave. Dora listened intently and said, "Of course, as soon as Jake finishes dinner, you can leave."

Tim heard what she said and responded "I'll get the wagon for them." He ate quickly and headed to the foyer.

Dora explained to the family, "Ethyl and Jake are helping out at a client's home over the holiday."

Jake stood and picked up his plate. "I'm finished. I'll go get ready to leave."

"Amy," Dora said, "we'll clear if you want to go ahead and go home. You shouldn't be out too late in this weather."

"I'll walk her over," Cole said. He started to take his plate to the kitchen.

Emma looked at Dora with raised eyebrows. Dora shrugged. First, the gifts from Paris, and now walking her home.

Amy took it and said, "I'll put it in the kitchen for you."

"Thank you. Meet me in the foyer?"

"I will," she said and headed back into the kitchen. She told everyone goodbye and went to the foyer to join Cole.

Jake called out, "Ethyl, Tim is here."

"Coming!" Ethyl hurried through the dining room. The family heard the door open and close. They continued to eat their dinner. Dora laughed at Lottie's antics with her food and turned to her father and stepmother. "Abbey, Papa, when you're finished, could you take Lottie and Patrick into the sitting room?"

"I can help," Henrietta spoke up. She jumped up from her chair and moved to the giggling Lottie. Patrick also got up and walked to the sitting room with Ellis and Abbey.

Jeremy, Emma, and Dora cleared the table and took everything into the kitchen. Each took a position to clean; Emma washed, Jeremy dried, and Dora put the items up. It didn't take long and, after a final wipe down, they plated the cookies. Dora directed, "Jeremy, grab the pitchers of punch we made earlier." He reached into the ice box and retrieved the pitcher.

"I have napkins and plates," Emma said as she moved to the door with a tray. Dora followed closely behind with another tray.

They went into the living room. Amy had popped the popcorn earlier and the cranberries were in a bowl sitting on the table with twine beside it.

Dora set everyone on the task of setting up for Christmas. Henrietta had moved to the tree, carrying Lottie. She reached out tentatively to touch it. "We never had a tree."

Dora heard her low voice and wiped the tears away as quickly as possible and went to give Patrick a box of ornaments. Jeremy and Emma sat with the twine to string the popcorn and cranberries. The door slammed open in the foyer and Tim appeared with a big grin.

"You couldn't wait for me?"

"Pa, we just started!" yelled Patrick. "Come help me with the tree."

Tim shrugged out of his coat and threw it on the table outside the sitting room. He knew he had to go back out and pick up Ethyl and Jake in a few hours.

CHAPTER 18

At Geoff and Gregory's apartment

Tim pulled up in front of the building and stopped. Jake jumped down and helped Ethyl to the sidewalk. Since they'd started the job together, Jake had been watching out for her, making sure she got in and out of the wagon safely.

Tim nodded and called over the wind, "I'll be back at the normal time to pick you up." Ethyl took Jake's hand and they ran into the building.

They checked in with the security guards and went up the elevator. The operator opened the door and waved them into the hallway. They stopped at the door and knocked; the instructions they were given indicated they always had to knock. In just a few moments, the door opened and Geoff stood there. He was dressed casually with no jacket. "Come in. The dishes are in the kitchen and we have the decorations for you to start putting out."

They went through their normal duties; Ethyl cleaned the

kitchen and Jake started to dust the area. As usual, music filled the apartment; Gregory was already at the piano playing. He normally played the entire time they were working in the home.

As Jake moved around the room, he silently documented all of the furniture they'd seen each night. This night, he noticed something new. "A trunk. This was not here last night," he muttered.

"What did you say?" Geoff asked. When Jake didn't respond, Geoff went back to his book.

Jake shook his head and continued to move through the room. As he did, his eyes kept getting drawn back to the trunk. *Emma will want to know about that.* He finished his dusting and went to help Ethyl clean the bathroom and straighten the bedrooms. Once he joined her in Geoff's bedroom, he turned to Ethyl.

"There's new furniture."

"Shh," she admonished him. "Show me when we start decorating. Right now, we need to finish in here." They changed the sheets and finished Geoff's and Gregory's bedrooms. Next, they moved to the boxes sitting in the foyer. She and Jake carried them into the living room.

Geoff sat reading, paying them little attention, and Gregory was at his piano. Ethyl knew after the first few days that they were to do their job with little interaction. She looked around the room and saw the tree was in the corner; her eyes found the trunk that Jake had mentioned. She made a mental note of the size. *Why is it here? It doesn't fit into the rest of the room. It's a travel trunk, and it's not one meant for the living areas.*

The duo unpacked the boxes of decorations and she sent Jake over to the tree to start hanging the ornaments. "Try to move them apart some," she said in a low voice. Jake nodded and started hanging them. She walked to the trunk and started to open it.

"Stop! What're you doing!" Geoff fairly screamed.

She stopped and turned to him slowly. "I was, uh, thinking to use this for the decorations we don't put out."

"Don't touch that trunk! It isn't to be used for storage!"

She backed away from it and said, "Yes, sir."

"Get back to work."

She walked back to the decorations and started to pull out some candles. Fresh garland had been delivered and she started to unwrap it.

Geoff's eyes followed her around the room. She tried to ignore the extra attention. As the decorations continued to go up, his interest lagged and he went back to his book. Ethyl almost sighed but continued to work.

The garland was placed around the room and candles were arranged. There were few comments from the two men the entire time. Ethyl looked around and asked Jake, "Would you move the empty boxes to the foyer?" Jake started doing so. "Mr. Beeker, will you have them moved back to storage?" Ethyl inquired.

Geoff didn't look up and said, "Tell the guard downstairs we need them moved."

"Yes, sir."

Ethyl and Jake started to leave. Geoff called to her, "Ethyl."

She turned, startled. It was the first time he'd used her name. "Yes, sir?"

"On the day of the party, we won't need you until the early afternoon."

"Oh," she said, surprised. "I'd planned on the morning to freshen the place up and get dinner ready."

"Early afternoon and no earlier, do you understand?"

"Yes, sir. I have the menu with the ingredients. Would you like me to shop for them?"

He looked bored again and said, "We have accounts set up. Just charge them to me."

"Yes, sir."

She and Jake gathered up their coats and left, making as little noise as possible. The silence continued as they made their way to the elevator. They rode down and gave the security guard the message about the empty boxes. He nodded and called to another guard nearby.

Jake said, "Tim will be waiting."

"Yes. Jake?" He paused, glancing at her. "Can you get off from work to help us with the shopping the day of the party?"

He looked conflicted but he'd do anything for Ethyl. "I'll ask for my vacation for that day."

"Good."

They took a few more steps and Ethyl said, "That trunk was odd."

"Yes," he said. "It was out of place, different, and didn't match the room."

"Mr. Beeker also got upset when I tried to open it."

"Yes."

"It's just odd." She mulled that over as they exited the building. Tim was huddled down on the wagon seat, waiting. They hurried over and Jake helped Ethyl into the driver's seat and climbed in the back. Tim nodded approvingly and clicked his tongue at the horse to move on.

They went to Ethyl's apartment first; she lived with her cousins and they'd all moved to the city together. Jake jumped down and helped her to the ground. When he started back up, she held his arm and moved his scarf down to reveal his lips. He started to complain when she lowered hers also and kissed him. "Thank you, Jake." She turned and headed into the building.

Jake stood there watching her once she'd gone in. After a few minutes, Tim tried to get his attention. "Jake? Jake! Come on, climb up, it's cold out here."

Jake nodded and joined Tim on the seat. Tim clicked his tongue and the horse started to move. They'd take her back to the warm stable for the night and then walk home. "Has that happened before?" Tim asked curiously.

"What?" Jake asked, his voice sounding distant.

"Ethyl kissing you?"

Jake sat and didn't say anything. Tim figured he was unconformable with the question and didn't ask another. They got to the stable and Tim unhooked the horse. Jake opened the door and they got the horse settled in a pen.

On their walk home, Jake said, "No." Tim knew that he was answering a question from earlier. He'd been thinking the whole time about this answer. "It was nice."

"Was it?"

"Yes." Jake looked over at Tim. "Does Dora kiss you?"

"Oh, yes. Often."

"And you like it?"

"Oh, yes. I surely do. Did you?"

"I think so."

Tim smiled. "Well, I hope she does it again."

"So do I."

Tim put his arm around Jake and laughed out loud. He continued as they walked the three blocks to the boarding house.

CHAPTER 19

partment-after Jake and Ethyl left.

Gregory knocked off the candle that had been placed on his piano. It fell to the floor and rolled toward Geoff. He stopped it with his foot.

"Why did she touch the trunk?" Gregory asked.

"Her answer made sense, and you see we have several items that have to go to storage. After all," he chided, "aren't trunks normally used for storage?"

Gregory walked over to the trunk. "I guess."

"You need to relax, Gregory. Everything's going as planned."

"Have you sent the note over?"

"I have and Ethan should receive it first thing in the morning."

"You think he'll come?"

"I know he will." He smiled. "I've worked everything out to the T. No one will be able to figure this out."

Gregory's mouth was drawn down and he kicked the trunk petulantly.

"Don't look like that, old man. We'll be doing this for you."

Gregory looked over angrily. "This isn't for me! This is all just to prove you can beat Emma. That you're smarter than her!"

"Hm," Geoff said, sounding bored with the conversation.

Gregory knew that response and went back to his piano.

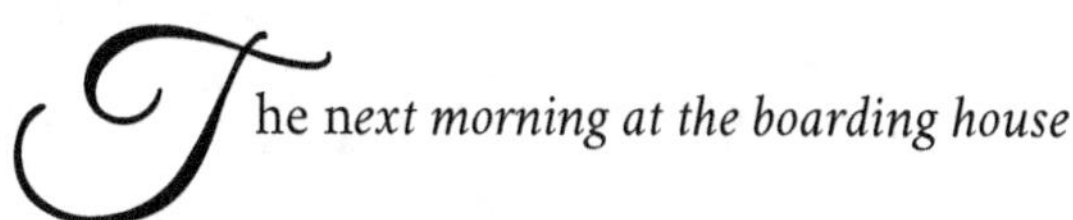

he next morning at the boarding house

Ethyl watched the kitchen door.

Amy noticed her focus and asked, "Who are you waiting for? Jake?"

"Yes. No. I don't know." She sputtered turning red. "I need to talk to Emma about the party."

"I mentioned the day off you need for that day to Dora. She was okay with it."

"That's good," Ethyl murmured and kept watching the door.

Amy let it go. As long as Ethyl got her work done, she wouldn't question her. They didn't have to wait long. Emma and Henrietta walked in together. "Good morning," Emma said brightly.

"Good morning. Breakfast will be ready soon," Amy said.

"Good, I'm hungry," Henrietta said.

"Last day of school for the holiday?" asked Amy.

"Yes, though I'll miss it," Henrietta replied, frowning.

"Hey, cheer up," Emma told the girl. "Why don't we stop by the bookstore on the way to the bakery today and you can pick out some reading for the holiday."

"That would be great!" A sudden scream caused them to start.

"I think Lottie's up," Amy said wryly.

"Yay!" said Henrietta. "Can I go play with her before breakfast?"

"Check with Dora!" Emma called. Henrietta had already run into the dining room. They heard the scream again, followed by giggling. "Sounds like she found her," Emma said with a smile.

"I think Ethyl wanted to talk with you," Amy said.

Emma leaned against the table, picked up an apple, and took a bite. "What is it?"

"I wanted to tell you about the job last night," Ethyl said in a low voice.

Emma smiled. "I don't think we have to whisper. Amy knows we're concerned about that party." Amy nodded and continued to roll out the biscuits.

"Okay, they've added a piece of furniture."

"Furniture? What's unusual about that?"

"It's a trunk."

"Like for traveling?"

"Yes, and quite old."

"Why does it bother you?"

"It was in the main sitting room and, when I attempted to open it, Mr. Beeker told me I wasn't to touch it."

"Does he normally direct you that way?"

"No, he normally ignores us." Emma mulled that over. "Is it important? I thought it might be important."

"I think so, though I don't know why." Emma took her apple, thinking about what Ethyl said. The party was tomorrow night. *What should we expect?*

he night of the party

There was no time to do anything but get ready. Dressing would take time and the women had washed their hair earlier that day in preparation. Emma, Dora, and Savannah were getting dressed in the fourth-floor sewing room.

"Will Ethan meet us here?" Dora asked, putting pins into her sister's hair. Emma sat in front of the mirror, sitting patiently while her hair was finished. The women were wearing updos with curls.

"No," Savannah said absently, curling her hair with a hot iron. A kerosene lamp was being used to provide the heat. "He has to pick up some things for Mr. Pennington. He'll join us there."

Tim called through the door, "Ladies, it's time to leave."

"We'll be down in a moment," called Dora. The house was rather quiet; the kids had been picked up by Clair's husband,

Thomas. Jake and Ethyl were already at the party. Savannah's parents had indicated they'd meet them there as well.

"All finished," Dora said, fixing stray hairs on Emma's head.

"Let me check yours," Emma said. Dora turned. "It looks good."

Dora walked over to Savannah. "Do you need any help?"

"No, I have it."

They already had their dresses on and, once their hair and makeup were in place, they started to leave. Emma hesitated by the dresser and picked up her smaller knife.

Dora saw her pick it up. "You think you'll need that? This is a party. Are you going to stab someone for getting too many hors d'oeuvres?"

Emma looked at the knife. "I might." She would've liked to bring it, but instead, she laid it down.

"Ready?" asked Savannah.

The sisters nodded and Emma walked over to open the door. The three exited, their dresses swishing as they moved down the stairs. Jeremy and Tim stood at the bottom, watching the lovely picture they made as they descended together.

Tim stepped up to Dora. "You look beautiful," he said and gave her a kiss. He looked at Emma and Savannah. "All of you look wonderful."

"I would have to agree," Jeremy said. He handed each of them their coats and scarves. Hats would be left behind tonight. Once dressed, he offered an elbow to both Emma and Savannah.

They laughed and started out. *We haven't been to a party in a long time. Maybe this will be fun,* thought Emma. One small thought floated through her head, though. *That trunk. What role is it going to play tonight?*

CHAPTER 22

*J*eremy and Emma's carriage stopped at Geoff and Gregory's building. Jeremy got out and then lifted Emma down to the snow-covered ground. Tim, Dora, and Savannah's carriage was a little behind them. Their group had split up into different carriages, so the dresses wouldn't be crumpled. Emma and Jeremy walked quickly into the building.

They waved to the guard; he'd been told they'd be arriving for the party. The elevator operator waited for them to make their way across the large lobby. *Will it be just us?* thought Emma. She didn't like to enter a situation where she wasn't aware of all the players. The group was quiet as the elevator rose to Geoff's floor. They walked to the door of Geoff and Gregory's apartment and she took a breath, watching as Jeremy raised his hand to knock.

The door opened and Ethyl stood there in a black dress and white apron. "Good evening. Are you here for the party?" She was still acting like she didn't know them.

"I'm Jeremy Tilden and this is Emma Evans," Jeremy replied.

She waved them in and took their coats. "Mr. Beeker and Mr. Walker are in the sitting room. This way, please."

They followed along behind Ethyl and, when they entered, they saw Gregory at the piano. He wasn't playing but, instead, his head was lowered and he appeared to be studying the keys. Geoff saw them and walked over.

"Is he ok?" Jeremy asked, indicating Gregory. The man still hadn't looked toward them.

Geoff laughed loudly. "Ignore Gregory. He has a performance coming up and gets quite introspective. Emma, Jeremy, we're so glad you could join us."

Jeremy shook his hand. "Thank you for the invite."

"Yes, thank you. You don't normally have these in Chicago?" Emma asked, keeping her voice light.

Jeremy was curious about Geoff's answer to that question.

"No, we move them every few years, don't we, Gregory?"

Gregory looked sullen but turned toward them and finally acknowledged their presence. "Yes, we like to have an influx of new people. Keeps the conversations interesting." He turned back to his piano, and once again ignored them.

Geoff shrugged. "Let's let Gregory be. Would you like a drink?" They walked to a small table that was set up as a bar on the other side of the piano.

A knock sounded at the door. Geoff looked torn; he wanted to go greet the new guest, but he wanted to stay and chat with Emma and Jeremy.

Jeremy noticed his indecision. "We can handle this if you want to greet your guests."

"Thank you," Geoff said as he handed the bottle to Jeremy and walked toward the door.

Dora and Tim entered with Savannah following closely behind. Gregory perked up when he saw her and left the piano to go greet them.

Emma observed the group at the door and said in a low voice to Jeremy, "Gregory's up."

Jeremy glanced over. "He only seems to be interested in Savannah."

"She doesn't look happy."

The closer Gregory got to her, the more uncomfortable she looked. She tried to back away from him.

"Call her over here," he suggested.

"Savannah," Emma called, "come join us for a drink." Savannah nodded gratefully and walked past Gregory to get to them.

Emma handed her a drink. "Thank you," Savannah muttered, taking a sip.

Gregory appeared to be lost without Savannah and started to move back to his piano. Before he could get there, they heard another knock on the door. Ethyl opened the door and Savannah's parents came into the room. Since the wedding preparations had begun, they'd been to dinner at the boarding house multiple times. Gregory looked happy to see them and, after Ethyl took their coats, they walked into the room together. Savannah went to join her parents, using them as a buffer between herself and Gregory.

"Well, so far, we know everyone," murmured Jeremy as he took a sip of his drink.

"Yeah," Emma said, looking around and tapping her glass with her ring. Her eyes found the anomaly in the room. It was the trunk. "Ethyl's right; it doesn't fit."

"What?" asked Jeremy, following her gaze to the trunk. "That's a little strange."

"Exactly. It's out of place." They walked toward it.

Gregory excused himself, went to stand by Geoff, and whispered furiously, "They're going to the trunk."

"Relax. It's just a trunk. They have nothing to be suspicious about," he said and took a drink.

"But—"

Geoff interrupted him. "See to our guests."

Gregory nodded and walked to Savannah's parents. The conversation revolved around their theatre shows. "When is your performance, Gregory?"

"Next month," he said, watching Emma out of the corner of his eye.

"He needs to practice more," Geoff said, moving to stand between Gregory and Emma, effectively blocking his view.

"Yes," Gregory commented, "we're planning to leave tonight to go to my home in the country. I'll be able to concentrate on my music there."

"See anything unusual?" Jeremy asked in a low voice as they tried to study the trunk unobtrusively.

Emma started to walk around the trunk to get a better look and Geoff said, "Emma, come join us. We were talking about the case that brought us together." She reluctantly stopped her evaluation and accompanied Jeremy over to Geoff.

Conversations flowed through the room: theatre, foundation work, and more. All the while, Geoff stared at the front door. Jake, dressed in a black suit, white shirt, and black tie, passed out hors d'oeuvres. Savannah took one from him but didn't eat it; she turned it over and over again in her hands. She looked worried.

"He'll be here soon," her mother reassured her.

"I knew he might be late, but not this late. Do you think something happened to him?" she asked.

Ethyl came up to Geoff and whispered into his ear. He shook his head in response and continued to stare at the door. He seemed to be waiting for someone.

An additional guest? thought Emma.

Gregory went over to Geoff, tugging on his arm. Geoff shook him off. Gregory lifted his hand to try again and, at that moment, a knock sounded on the door. Geoffe smiled broadly.

"Ah, Savannah, that's probably Ethan now." He went to answer it himself, waving Ethyl off.

"See, there he is now," Mrs. Wood said. Savannah smiled and followed Geoff to the door.

Geoff opened it, but it wasn't Ethan.

"John! So nice to see you. Come in," said Geoff.

Savannah's smile fell and she walked back to her parents. The entire room came to a standstill; the only people to not recognize the man were Savannah's parents. "Who is it?" Mrs. Wood asked.

"Juh-John Harden," stuttered Savannah. Her thoughts were on Ethan. *Where is he? Should I go to his office and check on him?*

Dora turned to Emma. "John Harden! What's he doing here?"

Jeremy finally turned his gaze from John and looked at Emma. "Are you okay?"

"I'm fine," she said shortly. *Something is going on, but what is it?* she asked herself and looked around at the other guests. "I already knew he was in town."

"You didn't mention it," he said, his voice going hard.

"What was I supposed to say, 'Oh, hey, Jeremy, John Harden the master criminal is in town and, by the way, he's a client of my boss. And because of the whole lawyer-client confidentiality thing, I was told to keep it to myself."

Jeremy understood that and murmured, "I'm sorry."

"That's okay. It was hard to keep this from you."

"So, why him and with this mix of people?"

Emma looked around, seeing what he saw. "Yeah, he's an unknown. I don't know how he knows anyone here, aside from us. And what's our part in this chess game?"

"Any ideas?"

"I'm not sure yet," she said as she studied John. "Let's go say hello." He looked surprised but went along with her.

They walked over and waited for a break in Geoff and John's conversation.

"Hello, John."

"Emma. Jeremy. I didn't know you'd be here," he stated and looked over at Geoff.

"I thought it might be a nice surprise," Geoff said, smiling.

"Did you know?" John responded.

Jake gestured to Geoff. Geoff announced, "Dinner is served." Jeremy, Emma, and John turned to him and frowned. "Well, it is. Let's head into the dining room," he said and tried to guide them into the room.

The group didn't move. "I don't know where Ethan has gotten to," Savannah said. "He should be here by now."

"Didn't he say he'd be late?" Mr. Wood asked.

"He did. He said he had a few errands." Savannah suddenly remembered something. She turned to Geoff. "He said was stopping by here. You asked him to come by this morning."

"Me? No, I didn't see him." He turned to Gregory and asked, "Did you see Ethan today?"

"No. I did expect him to drop off some contracts for my performance, but he hasn't come by. I was hoping to get them this evening before we left."

Geoff waved them into the dining room. Savannah continued to frown as her father and mother escorted her. Mr. Wood patted the hand resting on his elbow and reassured her. "I'm sure he'll be here soon." She nodded but didn't say anything.

John offered Emma his elbow. She shrugged and took it. *What the hell?* she thought. He held her chair and sat next to her. Jeremy started to protest. "It's okay, dear one," she said.

He frowned at John but didn't say anything as he sat on the other side of her. Across from them were Gregory and Geoff. Savannah and her parents were on the left, and Tim and Dora were on the right.

Jake and Ethyl brought the plates from the kitchen in an efficient manner. Everyone had their food and started to eat. Emma moved her food around her plate and asked John, "How do you know Geoff?"

"He's my accountant."

With eyebrows raised, she looked at Geoff.

"I do have other clients," he said. "John is just one of them."

"How long has he been a client?" she demanded.

John answered for him. "That's a business matter and not meant for this party."

Emma whispered furiously at him, "Did you know I'd be here?"

"No," he replied in a low voice. "Did you know I'd be here?"

"No."

They both looked at Geoff. He grinned widely at them, enjoying his dinner. Emma turned her gaze to Gregory; he didn't have the same smile. He avoided her gaze, looking down or looking toward Savannah. *How can two men be so different? What's Geoff orchestrating?* she thought.

Dinner conversation flowed about the latest plays and Gregory's upcoming performance. After dinner, everyone started moving back to the living room. Emma turned to Jeremy. "I'll be a moment."

"Do you need me to stay?"

"No, I have this."

He nodded and walked back into the sitting room.

She snagged Geoff by the arm and moved him into the kitchen. "What's going on?" she demanded.

Geoff looked scared for a moment but managed to calm himself down. "Nothing's going on. It's just a party," he responded.

"A party that includes me and John Harden."

"I didn't think it would be a problem," he said innocently.

She squinted at him and said reluctantly, "Maybe it's just a coincidence."

"Of course, that's all it was. Please excuse me, I must attend to my other guests."

He walked out and she stayed where she was. Emma noticed Ethyl and Jake were in the room. "You know, they've been acting oddly today," Ethyl said.

"And before," said Jake.

"What do you mean?"

"We weren't allowed to come in to clean and set up for dinner until after noon today," said Ethyl.

"Was anything different when you got here?"

"It was dark," Jake said.

"Dark? What do you mean dark? Inside, outside?"

"The curtains were all pulled closed in the sitting room areas," explained Ethyl.

"Is that normal?"

"No," she said. "Even at night, the curtains have been pulled back."

"Mr. Walker didn't want them open," Jake said.

"Mr. Beeker did, so we opened them," said Ethyl.

Emma mulled this over and went back to join the party.

Savannah stood by her parents. "I know something has happened to him." She glanced anxiously at the clock and twisted a handkerchief in her hands. She was getting frantic and close to tears.

Dora and Tim stood with Jeremy, and Emma joined them. "Did you find out why John is here?" Jeremy asked.

" Geoff says it's a coincidence. I don't believe him."

Jeremy said, "Yeah, me neither."

John sat on a settee with his drink and took the dessert Ethyl offered. "Well, my dear, something is going on here tonight."

She nodded and looked at Geoff and Gregory. "They're more extreme tonight."

"How so?" he asked, watching them.

"Mr. Beeker is more jovial and Mr. Walker is more morose."

"Hmm," John said, taking a bite of his dessert.

Geoff came and joined him on the settee. "Are you having a nice time?" he asked with a wide smile.

" Geoff, I'm unhappy that I'm here as a pawn tonight."

"Surely not a pawn, John. You're so much more than that," Geoff commented and then stood and walked over to Savannah and her parents.

John moved over to Emma where she stood with her group. "Emma, you're right, we're being used. And I think we need to do something about it."

"Finally! What're you planning, John?" she asked.

"What I do best, of course," he commented wryly.

"That's more than a little alarming," Jeremy said with a raised eyebrow.

John smiled a wolfish smile as he moved to join Gregory on the bench. Gregory started to protest at the intrusion but then saw who it was. He turned back to the music and continued to play.

"What's going on, Gregory?" John asked quietly.

"I don't know what you're talking about." John heard the error when his fingers hit the wrong keys.

"Your nerves are showing," he observed. Gregory kept playing.

"Gregory, what's Geoff planning?" he asked. Gregory laughed at that and sounded more relaxed. "Hmm, looks like I'm wrong. How about I ask what Geoff has already done?"

Gregory tried to continue playing, but the errors piled up. He finally slammed the lid down on the keys and stood up rather quickly. " I need a drink." He stormed off to the small bar and poured himself a tall drink. John watched him.

Gregory drank his drink quickly and poured another. He watched, horrified, as Emma and Jeremy walked back to the trunk to study it again. Gregory ran to Geoff and whispered furiously in his ear, "They know something!"

"They know nothing," said Geoff. "Now calm down and stop drinking."

"I'll do what I want, just like you do," he said defiantly and quickly drank his new drink and walked back to make another.

"Something's got Gregory spooked," Emma observed.

"Yeah, and John's conversation didn't seem to help," Jeremy said.

Emma looked down at the trunk and walked around it slowly. "This is the key, I know it is." She saw a rope hanging out of the trunk. *Why is that there?* She eased Jeremy in front of her and, when he was in place, she grabbed the rope and pulled it. There was some resistance but it finally gave, and she slipped it into her pocket. *For later,* she thought. She moved to his side, took his drink, and took a sip.

"What was it?" he asked.

"A clue."

"But a clue to what?"

Geoff wandered over. "Why the interest in the old trunk?"

"We were wondering the same about you. Why is it here?" Jeremy asked.

"Well, I know Emma is interested in first-edition books. We found some at the New York house and used this to move them," Geoff explained.

"That's a lot of trunk for some books," Emma commented. "Are they still in there? I'd like to see them," she said and moved to open it up.

"No, no," assured Geoff. "I have them on the shelves in my bedroom. We can go look at them now if you like."

She gave him a long look and then turned to Jeremy. "Are you joining us?"

"You go on. I think I'll stay here." She nodded and followed Geoff.

Jeremy turned to stare at the trunk. John walked over to him and handed him a drink. "Are you enjoying yourself?"

Jeremy smiled without humor and said, "We're somehow involved in a play of Geoff's making."

"I was thinking more of a chess game and Emma's the queen. She's valuable because the queen can move in several directions. This makes the queen a useful piece that can be used for annihilating other players on the board."

"Then you think this is somehow about Savannah?" Jeremy looked over at her; she was crying and watching the door. "Do you think they did something to Ethan?"

"I think so. Whatever it is, seems to have already happened."

"John, why are you here? Did you know Emma would be here?"

"No," John admitted, "I've moved on with my life and all debts between us are settled. I came here at the invitation of a friend. Or so I thought."

Savannah's parents walked over. "Savannah is too upset to stay," Mr. Wood said. "She wants to go find out if Ethan's okay. I'm sure he is, but you know with the wedding so close, her nerves are on edge."

"Of course," Jeremy said. "Let us know if you need anything." He walked over to bid Savannah goodbye and saw Tim and Dora pulling on their coats.

"We're going also," Tim said. "It's getting late and we have babies that need to be picked up and put to bed." He looked over at Jeremy and said, "We will get Henrietta to bed also."

"Thanks," said Jeremy gratefully.

Gregory watched their guests getting ready to leave and fairly screamed, " Geoff!"

Geoff came out of the bedroom in a rush but tried to appear nonchalant. "What's going on? It's early yet."

"I need to find Ethan," Savannah said. "It's been too long since I heard from him."

"We're also going with her," her father said. Her mother agreed.

"We'll be going also," Dora said, coming up behind the Woods.

"Then I can't stop you, but I can help you with your things."

Geoff retrieved their coats and hats. Emma moved to join John and Jeremy by the trunk. Jeremy handed her a drink as they watched the room empty.

"Well, what now?" asked Jeremy.

"I don't know, but he's lost part of his audience," John commented.

"I think the next move is ours," said Jeremy.

Emma didn't respond. Instead, she laid down her drink and reached into her pocket. She started running the rope through her fingers.

"Gun," muttered Jeremy. " Geoff has it in his pocket." He watched Geoff put his hand into his pocket.

"Not to worry," John said in a similar tone. "So do I." He waited patiently, not pulling it out.

Geoff walked over to them with Gregory trailing behind. "You seem to be getting along very well," he said with a slight frown.

"Why does that bother you?" Emma asked.

"I think that he expected me to play the part of combatant," said John.

"Cat and mouse; which is the cat, which is the mouse?" Gregory asked desperately.

Jeremy interrupted the wordplay. " Geoff, what's going on here? Did you and Gregory do something to Ethan?"

"Whatever led you to that conclusion?" Geoff asked, laughing. Gregory spotted the rope in Emma's hand and whispered furiously to him. Geoff responded by putting his hand into his pocket.

"There's the gun you're gripping that leads me to that

conclusion," Jeremy commented, "and bringing John in as a distraction to Emma."

John's face was rock hard at this comment. He didn't like to be used.

At that moment, a knock sounded on the door. The five of them didn't move. Ethyl went to open the door and people stepped in; Dora, Tim, Savannah's parents, Savannah, and surprisingly, Ethan!

"Guess who we found when we got downstairs?" Savannah explained. She was laughing and crying in excitement. "He had just arrived. He was working late."

"I'm sorry if I provided any stress to the evening," Ethan said.

Geoff and Gregory stared at him, shocked. Geoff shook it off first. "Ethan?" he asked wonderingly.

"Yes, I'm sorry to be late."

"That's fine, that's fine," Geoff murmured, glancing at the trunk.

"It's not Ethan," murmured Emma, "but someone. Who?"

Ethan continued, "I hope you got your contracts from Julian here this morning Gregory."

Julian! Emma thought.

"Oh, you sent your cousin over with the papers?" asked Savannah.

"Your cousin?" said Gregory faintly and sat down abruptly on the settee.

"Jeremy, John. It's time," Emma said. They both grabbed Geoff and threw him to the floor. While they were securing him, Emma grabbed Gregory and twisted his arm. He was easily controlled and, while she was holding him down, Tim took a tie from the curtains and helped bind his hands together.

"Hey now, what kind of party is this?" Ethan asked, only half kidding.

Emma turned to him. "I think Julian is in that trunk. Have you heard from him after he delivered the papers today?"

"Trunk? What do you mean? Is he okay?"

She held out the rope to Geoff and said, "Answer the man's questions." Geoff looked mutinous. *I wish I'd brought my knife,* she thought.

Gregory burst out hysterically, "We got it wrong! It wasn't supposed to go this way!"

"They… they switched the players on me," Geoff stammered. "It has to be Ethan. It has to be."

"You just had to have her here, didn't you? You had to prove you were smarter than her," Gregory snarled at him.

"I am smarter," Geoff said desperately.

"Yeah, I don't think so," Jeremy said sarcastically.

Emma turned to the trunk. "It's time."

"No!" shouted Geoff. "Don't. I've worked too hard to beat you."

"We have to," said Emma.

John turned to the group. "You folks should turn around; this may not be pleasant." The women turned but Ethan stayed facing them. He had to know if Julian was in there.

Emma gripped the lid and opened it quickly. As expected, Julian was in there. The rest of the room reacted; Savannah and Ethan started to cry. *He still has color in his face,* she thought with a frown. *Why is that?* She bent down and touched his neck, feeling for a pulse. It was there, but barely. "I think he might be alive."

"What!" exclaimed Ethan and Geoff, both for very different reasons. Ethan ran over to the trunk.

"Let's get him out of there," Tim said. He, Jeremy, and Ethan lifted Julian out of the trunk and laid him on the settee.

"How is he alive?" Geoff asked, confused. "I don't understand it."

Ethan walked over to him and tightened his fist. "You son of a bitch!" he said and slugged the other man in the face. Geoff fell to the floor, unconscious.

Emma said, "Jake, we need help here. Can you run and get Sister Catherine at the hospital?"

"Yes. Should I bring the police?" he asked.

"That won't be necessary," Cole said from the door. "We have them with us."

Jeremy went over to them. "What's this, Pops?"

"Nathan said it was time to move; he has the data we needed and he was worried about the trip that Geoff and Gregory were going on. He didn't think they'd return."

"Gregory said they were just going to his country house."

"They were, by way of South America. Nathan found the travel plans." Cole handed Jeremy some papers. Jeremy stayed where he was and began reviewing them.

Emma was looking at the marks on Julian's neck and then at the rope in her hand. "Gregory, can you explain these markings to me?"

John hauled him up and moved the man closer to Emma. "I didn't want to hurt Savannah that way and kill her fiancé." Gregory started to cry.

"What did you do?" Geoff asked groggily from the floor.

"When Geoff got behind Julian with the rope, I put two fingers where his windpipe was and stopped it from being crushed. He passed out and Geoff naturally assumed he was dead."

"And you had it dark enough where Geoff couldn't tell he was still alive."

"Yes. I also cut a hole in the trunk so he could breathe."

"I just thought it was damaged," said Emma. She'd noticed the kicked-in hole.

"That's how I wanted it to look. "

"What were your plans after the party?"

"I didn't have any," Gregory admitted. "I couldn't think that far ahead. I just wanted Savannah to be mine."

Savannah moved closer to her parents and looked away from his gaze.

"Geoff, we know why Gregory was involved. Why were you?" asked Emma.

"You think you're so smart. I had plans for Millicent, but you uncovered her operation."

"Millicent? Millicent Carlisle? But she's the reason we now work together," said Emma. Millicent Carlisle was a murderess who Emma helped bring to justice. Afterward, Millicent's grandfather left Emma the money to start the foundation.

"The plan was for us to have all the money, and then somehow you ended up with it all and you were just giving it away," Geoff sneered.

"That was the young woman who killed all of her servants?" John asked.

Jeremy had walked back over and heard John's comment. He responded, "Yes, poison; it looked like she also killed her parents."

"She isn't around anymore?"

"She was hanged."

"Hmph. No big loss there."

"No."

Emma wanted one more answer from Geoff. "Was that you at Henrietta's school?"

Geoff looked mutinous.

Gregory answered, "It was him, he wanted you to be distracted and thought that would do it."

"It did," she commented. "And her parents,"

"Geoff paid them off."

Jeremy came over to her and said, "A good thing."

She nodded thinking of all the plans Geoff had just to beat her and prove he was smarter.

The Pinkertons, along with the police, took Geoff and Gregory into custody. Charges would be placed against them.

Emma went to Cole and whispered into his ear. Cole nodded and said, "I'll check into it."

As Geoff and Gregory passed Savannah, Gregory tried to catch her eye, but she turned her back to him. He hung his head and went willingly with the officers.

Sister Catherine arrived with Ethan and approved moving Julian. He'd started to regain consciousness.

Jake and Ethyl were taken home by Dora and Tim. Ethyl commented that they'd been paid upfront for their services. So, Ethyl had achieved her goal to save enough money for Jake's gift.

Once Emma, Jeremy, and John were alone in the apartment, John pulled three cigars and offered one to Emma and Jeremy. All three sat watching the smoke go up. "I guess we need a new accountant," John commented ruefully.

"Yeah," Emma agreed. "Jeremy, you think Nathan could stay on and help us find an honest accountant?"

"I think he can. I think he rather enjoyed the work."

John asked her, "Did you suspect anything before we got here tonight?"

"Not anything specific, just a feeling, but Geoff planned this when we had a lot of other activities going on."

"What were you saying to Pops?" Jeremy asked.

"Oh, that; I told him he might want to check the other parties Geoff and Gregory have had and see if there were trunks at those other parties."

CHAPTER 23

he *wedding*

It almost hadn't happened. But with everyone pitching in, they were ready for the wedding to begin. Emma and Dora were standing in the hallway, waiting for Savannah to exit her room with her father.

At that moment, the door opened and she stepped out. She was so lovely that tears formed in both Dora's and Emma's eyes. Emma blotted her eyes and handed a handkerchief to Dora to do the same.

"You look wonderful!" Dora said.

"It's the dress," Savannah said, beaming.

"No," said Emma, "it's all you. Are we ready?"

They nodded and Emma waved downstairs. The music started, they descended into the foyer, and turned into the living room. Emma saw Ethyl standing by Jake. When he leaned down to kiss her, Emma grinned. Once she and Dora made it to the front to wait for the bride, Dora asked her sister in a low voice, "Did I just see that?"

"Yes, you did. Isn't it wonderful?" They both turned to watch Savannah.

The bride stood in the arch of the door. Ethan stood across the room and waited for her to begin their life together. His best man, Julian, stood next to him. He still looked a little gray but he'd said he wouldn't miss the wedding. Ethan had suggested the wedding could be moved, but he refused. He said they tried to stop the wedding by killing him; he'd do anything to make sure Ethan ended up with Savannah.

Notebook Mysteries

Parisian
Intrigue

KIMBERLY
MULLINS

Notebook Mysteries

Books
1 - 2 - 3

KIMBERLY
MULLINS

ABOUT THE AUTHOR

Kimberly Mullins is the author of series of books titled "Notebook Mysteries". Her stories are based on historical events occurring in 1871-1890's Chicago. She holds a BS in Biology and a MBA in Business. She lives in Texas with her husband and son. When she is not writing she is working as a Process Safety Engineer at a large chemical company. You can connect with her on her website www.kimberlymullinsauthor.com.

Photo Credit: Blessings of Faith Photography

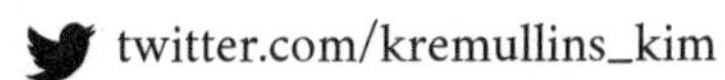

twitter.com/kremullins_kim